Herausgeber: Dr. Frank Haß

Blue | Red | Orange Line 4

Förderausgabe

Ernst Klett Verlag
Stuttgart · Leipzig · Dortmund

Inhalt

Zoom in

Welcome to the USA

1 Look at the map. Write the regions' names in the right places.
Schau dir die Karte an. Schreibe die Namen der Regionen an die richtigen Stellen.

South | Midwest | Northeast | Southwest ✓ | West

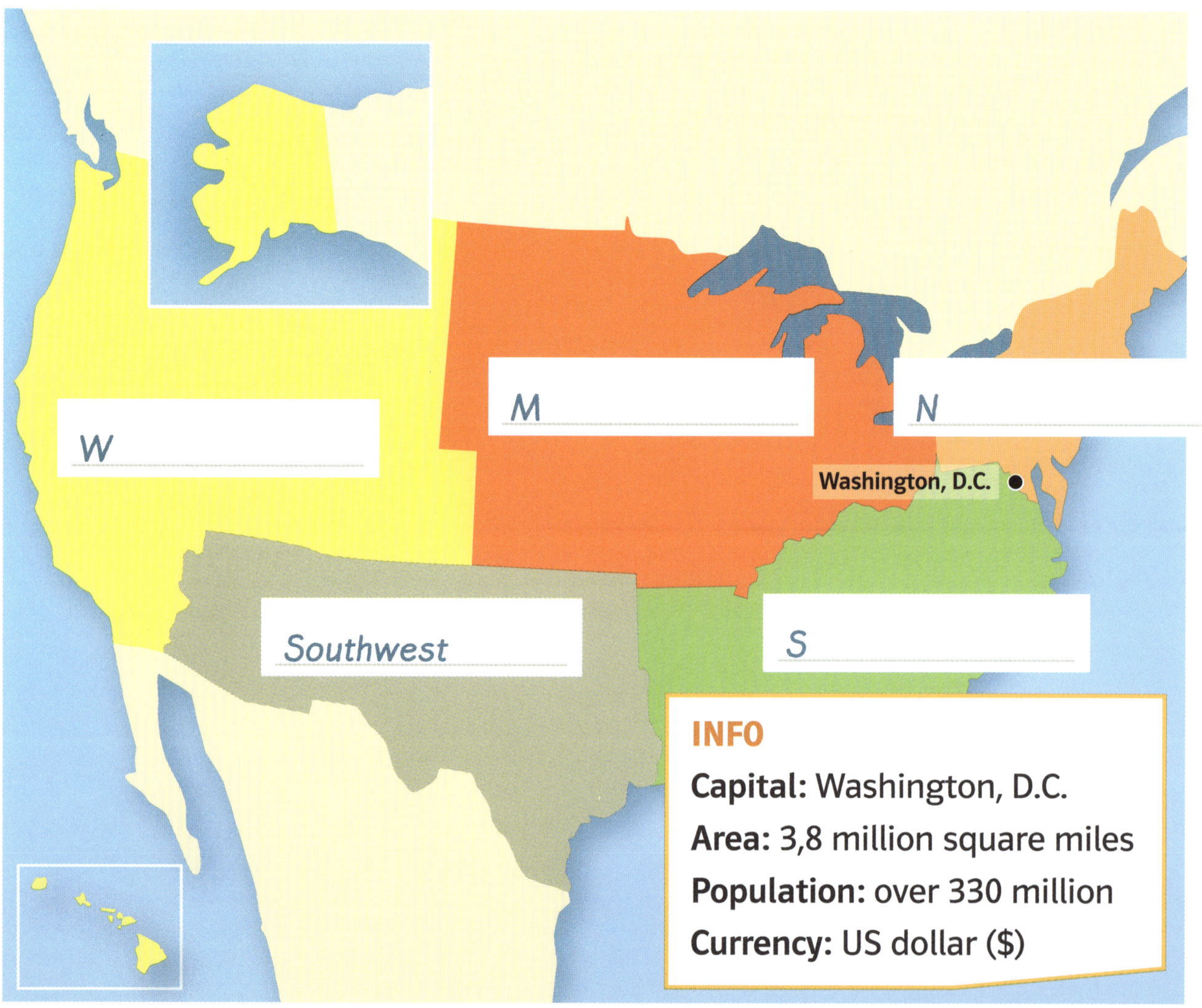

INFO

Capital: Washington, D.C.
Area: 3,8 million square miles
Population: over 330 million
Currency: US dollar ($)

Zoom in

2 What do you know about the USA? Talk to a partner.

Was weißt du über die USA? Sprich mit einem Partner oder einer Partnerin.

1. America's most famous city: N ________ Y ________ C ________
2. Number of states: f ________
3. Colours of the flag: b ________, w ________ and r ________
4. Colour of American school buses: y ________
5. Popular sports: b ________, b ________ and f ________
6. Popular food: h ________

3 Watch the film. Complete the information in exercise 2.

V 1

Schau dir den Film an. Vervollständige die Informationen in Übung 2.

4 Listen and tick the right boxes.

A 1

Höre zu und setze Häkchen bei den richtigen Kästchen.

1. Leo is from the ☐ Northwest. ☑ Northeast.
2. He wants to be a ☐ designer. ☐ tour guide.
3. Brad's city has a German festival every ☐ week. ☐ year.
4. Luciana ☐ chats ☐ plays with her friends online.
5. Julie lives near the ☐ mountains. ☐ lake.
6. Macy lives with her parents and her sister ☐ Becca. ☐ Charlie.

1 Arriving in the Northeast

In dieser Unit wirst du …
- etwas über den Nordosten erfahren.
- Sehenswürdigkeiten in New York City präsentieren.
- eine Dokumentation anschauen.
- über das Leben von Jugendlichen sprechen.
- ein Interview anhören.
- verschiedene Texte zu einem Thema lesen.

A

B

Niagara Falls and the Appalachian Mountains are some of the USA's most beautiful countryside.

INFO

Biggest city: New York City (NYC), about 8 million people
Highest point: Mount Washington

C

English settlers gave the cities names from home like Boston. Long before that, Native Americans lived there.

D

Between 1892 and 1954, around 12 million immigrants arrived on Ellis Island in New York Harbor.

E

The Northeast coast is great for whale watching from May to October.

F

Around 23 % of the USA's economy is in the Northeast. It's one of the richest areas of the USA.

1 Facts about the Northeast

a) Read the texts. Add the words to the notes.
Lies die Texte. Ergänze die Wörter auf den Notizzetteln.

Zwei Lücken bleiben frei. Die füllst du in Aufgabe 1 b) aus.

Native Americans ✓ | whale watching | New York City | rich area | immigrants | Niagara Falls

History
- Native Americans
-
- national

Cities
- New
-

Nature
- Appalachian Mountains
-
-

Economy – area

b) Watch the film. Circle the right answers and add them to the notes in a). Schau dir den Film an. Kreise die richtigen Antworten ein und ergänze sie in den Notizen in a).

V 2

1. The national **memorials** | **airports** are popular sights.
2. The capital city is **Washington, D.C.** | **Boston**.

c) Talk about the Northeast.
Sprich über den Nordosten.

Es hilft dir beim Vorlesen, wenn du die Sätze zuerst aufschreibst.

The Northeast is famous for whale watching.

Niagara Falls | its economy | its beautiful countryside | …

In the past Native Americans lived there.

English settlers lived | immigrants arrived | …

Today there are many big cities like New York City.

Philadelphia | Boston | …

✓ Ich kann Informationen über den Nordosten verstehen.

Sights in New York City

1 Read the blog post. Lies den Blogeintrag.

Internet

09/17/2025

New York, New York

Hi guys! I'm visiting New York this week with my friend Aya.

We started at the new platform **Edge** in Manhattan. It's on the side of a skyscraper with 100 stories. It has a glass floor, and the views are amazing. Aya used the stairs, but I took the elevator.

A

We walked on the **High Line** next. It's a beautiful park on an old train track. The park is about 27 feet above the streets and about 1.5 miles long. You can see the Statue of Liberty from there too.

B

After that we took the subway to the **Intrepid Museum**. That's a big museum ship on the Hudson River. It has many planes, a submarine, and a space shuttle. It was OK.

C

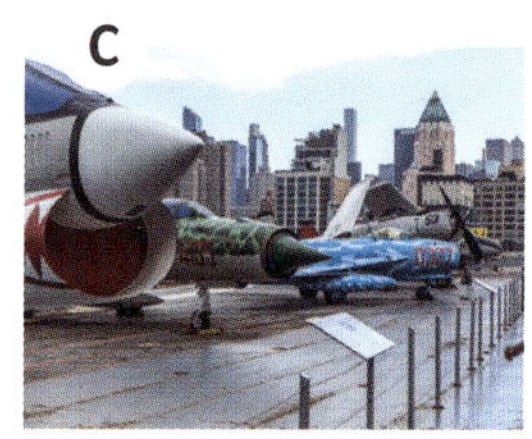

Then the highlight of my trip! We visited **Fifth Avenue**. Many of the world's greatest fashion stores are there. I looked at all the crazy fashion ideas. Aya thought it was a bit boring. Oh well … 😊

D

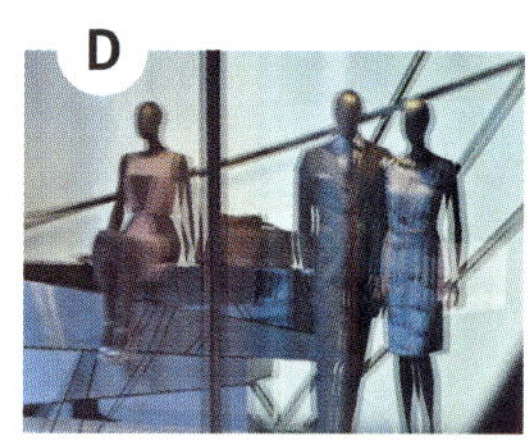

2 Sightseeing in New York

a) Are the sentences true or false? Tick.

Sind die Sätze wahr oder falsch? Setze Häkchen.

	true	false
1. You can look through the floor at Edge.	☐	☐
2. Leo and Aya cycled on the High Line.	☐	☐
3. Aya loved Fifth Avenue too.	☐	☐

b) Which of the places would you like to visit? Why?
Welche dieser Orte würdest du gerne besuchen? Warum?

A I'd like to visit Edge because I'd love to see the view of New York.

B I'd prefer to visit Fifth Avenue because I really like fashion.

the Intrepid Museum | the High Line | I like nice views | I love parks | museums are interesting | I like shopping | …

3 Parts of a building ► Vokabeln S.122 (V1)

a) Match the words with the right parts of the building.
Ordne die Wörter den richtigen Teilen des Gebäudes zu.

entrance | balcony | elevator | story | solar panels | ground level ✓ | stairs

b ______ s ______ s ______

ground level ______ e ______ e ______ s ______

Manche Dinge sind im amerikanischen Englisch (AE) anders als im britischen Englisch (BE):
elevator (AE) → lift (BE)
story (AE) → floor (BE)

b) Match the words with the definitions. What's the hidden word?
Ordne die Begriffe den Definitionen zu. Wie heißt das versteckte Wort?

1. ground level	where you go into a building	T
2. entrance	you can sit outside on this	O
3. balcony	the first floor of a building	S
4. elevator	you can walk up and down them	Y
5. stairs	it takes you to different floors	R

1	2	3	4	5
S				

4 Mediation: Answer the questions about the photo in German.
Sprachmittlung: Beantworte die Fragen zu dem Foto auf Deutsch.

In 1932 a newspaper showed this photo. You can see eleven men sitting on a steel beam eating their lunch. They are about 853 feet above the ground. The men were working on

the new building. The photographer asked them to sit like this because he wanted to promote the skyscraper. This is one of the most famous photos of New York City. It is a piece of American history.

1. Wie viele Männer sind auf dem Foto zu sehen? *Es sind elf.*
2. Was tun sie auf dem Stahlträger? *Sie essen*
3. Warum tun sie das? *Der Fotograf*

   weil
4. Was ist das Besondere an dem Foto? *Es ist*

Language

In der einfachen Vergangenheit werden **am**, **is** und **are** zu **was** und **were**:

I'**m** tired today. → I **was** tired yesterday.
Are you in New York? → **Were** you in New York?
How **is** your holiday? → How **was** your holiday?

Aus **do** wird **did**. Das brauchst du oft für Fragen:

Did they have lunch? What **did** he ask?

5 Choose the right words. Act the dialogue with a partner. Then change roles. Wähle die richtigen Wörter aus. Spielt den Dialog zu zweit. Dann tauscht die Rollen.

You Hi, how **was** | **is** your trip to New York?
Aya Hi. My trip to New York was great.
You When **does** | **did** you return?
Aya We returned yesterday.
You Who **is** | **was** with you?
Aya Leo was with me.
You **Do** | **Did** you visit Edge?
Aya Yes, we visited Edge.
You What **was** | **are** your highlight?
Aya My highlight was the Intrepid Museum.
You How **did** | **do** you get there?
Aya We took the subway there.

6 **Your turn:** A blog post about a sight in New York City

Write a blog post about a New York City sight.

Schreibe einen Blogeintrag über eine New Yorker Sehenswürdigkeit.

Step 1: Choose a sight in New York City.
Suche dir eine Sehenswürdigkeit in New York City aus.

– The Statue of Liberty
– Hudson Yards
– ...

Step 2: Search the internet for information.
Suche im Internet nach Informationen.
- Where? (Wo?)
- What? (Was?)
- Opening times? (Öffnungszeiten?)
- For free or buy tickets? (Kostenlos oder Tickets kaufen?)

Hudson Yards:
– on the west side near the Hudson River
– a great place to visit
– Vessel not open at the moment
– free
– ...

Step 3: Write a draft. Use hashtags for the places.
Schreibe einen Entwurf.
Benutze Hashtags für die Orte.

Media tip
Mit Hashtags (#) sind bestimmte Informationen leichter zu finden.
Beispiel: #VesselNY #NYsights

Step 4: Find one or more photos that you can add.
Finde ein oder mehr Fotos, die du hinzufügen kannst.

Step 5: Write your blog post and add the photos.
Schreibe deinen Post und füge die Fotos hinzu.

Visit Vessel Hudson Yards, NYC.
It's crazy!
Have you been here? Tell me.
#NewYork #VesselNY
#VesselNysights #crazystairs

✓ Ich kann Sehenswürdigkeiten in New York City präsentieren.

A sad but important day in New York

1 Match the English words with their German meaning.

Verbinde die englischen Wörter mit ihrer deutschen Bedeutung.

1. attack	flog
2. flew	der Anschlag
3. collapse	entführen
4. hijack	zusammenbrechen

2 Watch the film. Put the sentences in the right order.

V 3

Schau dir den Film an. Bringe die Sätze in die richtige Reihenfolge.

Media tip

Bilder von Gewalt und Katastrophen können Angst machen. Es ist wichtig, mit anderen darüber zu sprechen. Das kann helfen, weniger Angst zu haben.

A Thousands of people died in the attack. ☐

B They flew them into the World Trade Center. ☐

C New York built a memorial and a new skyscraper. ☐

D The two towers collapsed. ☐

E Terrorists hijacked two planes. 1

F About 700 emergency workers died too. ☐

3 How do people in New York remember the people who died in the attacks? Circle two more right answers.

V 3

Wie erinnern sich Menschen in New York an die Leute, die bei den Anschlägen gestorben sind? Kreise zwei weitere richtigen Antworten ein.

They built **a memorial** | **two waterfalls** | **planes** | **a new tower** | **a park**.

✓ Ich kann eine Dokumentation verstehen.

A day in the life of an American teenager

1 Read the website. Lies die Webseite.

Internet

Making new friends online

You are just a minute away from a new friend. Our teenagers are from many different places in the USA and around the world. They like to make new friends and chat about their lives and their favorite places. Read their posts and answer them.

Nicolas, 17, Waitsfield, Vermont

Hi guys, I'm Nicolas. I live in Waitsfield, a small town in Vermont. I go to Bloomfield High School. The school isn't my favorite place, but I love the sports grounds there.
I play lacrosse in spring and ice hockey in winter. It's great because I've made some good friends.
My favorite place is the best seafood restaurant in town. What's your favorite place?
Church is also a big part of my life. When my family moved here, the church really helped us to feel at home.
I like the fun activities for young people there on Sunday afternoons.

Logan, 16, Philadelphia, Pennsylvania

My name is Logan. My family and I live in a small apartment in Philadelphia.
I share a room with my two younger brothers. They're nosy, so I spend a lot of time on the basketball court.
That's my favorite place. I can play alone or with friends and I can forget all my problems there.
My other favorite place is the Magic Gardens arts center.
I get lots of ideas for my own art projects there.
Some people think it's crazy, but I love it.
Which place makes you happy?

2 Complete the table. Vervollständige die Tabelle.

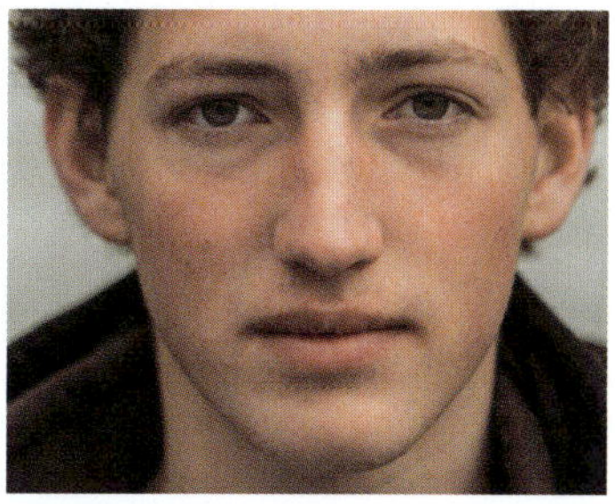

	Nicolas	Logan
Home	*Waitsfield*	
Activities		
Two favourite places		

3 Answer **one** of the posts.

Beantworte **einen** der Beiträge.

Hi ______________________, Nicolas/Logan

I'm ______________________ (dein Name)

from ______________________. (dein Wohnort)

I live in ______________________ a flat | a house

with my ______________________ parents | family | older sister

______________________. younger brother | dog | …

I go to ______________________. (deine Schule)

My favourite place is ______________________ my room | the gym | the forest

______________________. the café | the youth club | …

4 Talk about what you think of these things. ► Vokabeln S.123 (V2)

Sprecht darüber, wie ihr diese Dinge findet.

A

cat

B

decoration

C

truck

D
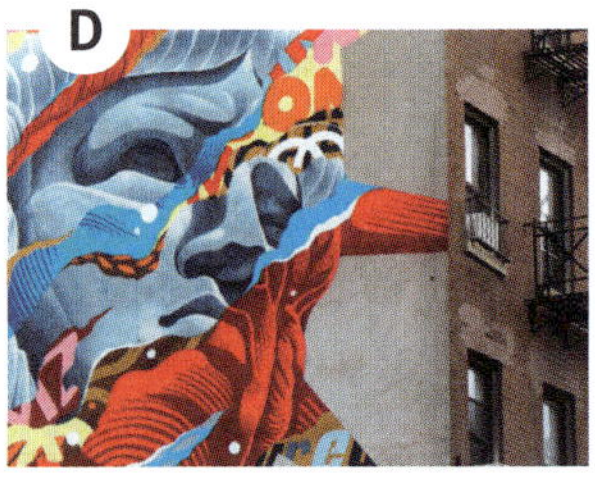
mural

A I think the cat is beautiful. great cool funny crazy …

B But I think it looks strange. boring dangerous scary …

5 Listen to the interview. Tick the right answers.

A 2

Höre dir das Interview an. Setze Häkchen bei den richtigen Antworten.

Culture
Die Amischen sind eine religiöse Gruppe. Sie verließen im 18. Jahrhundert Europa und gingen nach Nordamerika. Sie sprechen heute noch einen deutschen Dialekt.

1. Where does Bridget live?
   - ☐ She lives in a flat.
   - ☑ She lives on a farm.
2. When did Bridget leave school?
   - ☐ When she was 16.
   - ☐ When she was 15.
3. What does Bridget do most mornings?
   - ☐ She helps with the animals.
   - ☐ She looks after her brothers.
4. Why does she enjoy her job at the store?
   - ☐ She meets people.
   - ☐ She chooses what the store sells.
5. When do most Amish people use technology?
   - ☐ When they work in the garden.
   - ☐ When they wash their clothes.

Language
Du vergleichst Personen, Tiere und Dinge mit **er** und **than** nach dem Adjektiv:

Waitsfield is quiet**er** **tha**n Boston.

Wenn du sagen willst, dass etwas am besten, schönsten, schnellsten, … ist, setzt du **est** ans Wortende: „This is the high**est** building I've ever seen!"

6 Complete the sentences. Vervollständige die Sätze.

older ✓ | hotter | larger | noisier

I'm Zach and I work for a family in Italy. I look after two children, Matilda and Daniele, while their parents are at work.

Matilda is *older* ____________ than Daniele. I help them with their English.

My room is nice and it's ____________ than my room at home.

The family live in a busy area. It's much ____________ than where I live.

The summer here is much ____________ than in Boston too.

7 Compare the places. Say where you would rather live.

Vergleicht die Orte. Sagt, wo ihr lieber wohnen würdet.

more colourful | smaller | noisier | more exciting | dirtier | more boring | …

A

B

A I like Boston better. The city is larger and more interesting than Waitsfield.

B I prefer Waitsfield. It's nicer and cleaner than Boston.

A Maybe. But … .

B …

8 **Your turn:** A short video about your favourite place

Make a video about your favourite place.

Drehe ein Video über deinen Lieblingsort.

Step 1: What's your favourite place? What do you do there? Why is it important to you?
Was ist dein Lieblingsort? Was machst du da? Warum ist er dir wichtig?

– my grandma's garden
– help her with the flowers, the fruit and vegetables
– relax after school
– ...

Step 2: Make a short video about your favourite place.
Drehe ein kurzes Video über deinen Lieblingsort.

S **Skills**
Dein Video wird interessanter, wenn du aus verschiedenen Blickwinkeln filmst und unterschiedlich nah heranzoomst.

Step 3: Use an app on your tablet or phone to edit the video.
Benutze eine App auf deinem Tablet oder Smartphone, um das Video zu bearbeiten.

Step 4: Write a short text about the place and what you do there.
Schreibe einen kurzen Text über den Ort und was du dort tust.

Hi, this is my grandma's garden. I often help her with the flowers, fruit and vegetables. It's my favourite place because I can relax there after school. ...

Step 5: Record your text.
Nimm deinen Text auf.

Step 6: Put everything together and finish your video.
Füge alles zusammen und stelle dein Video fertig.

S **Skills**
Wenn du den Text für dein Video aufgenommen hast, höre ihn dir an und prüfe, ob man alles gut verstehen kann. Wenn nicht, nimm ihn nochmal neu auf.

✓ Ich kann über das Leben von Jugendlichen sprechen.

The American Dream

1 Read the text. Find the meanings of the underlined words.

Lies den Text. Schlage die Bedeutungen der unterstrichenen Wörter nach.

The American Dream says that you can achieve what you believe in. If you work hard, you can be successful. Many people immigrate to the USA because they want to have a better life.

1. to achieve – *erreichen* ______
2. to work hard – ______
3. successful – ______
4. to immigrate – ______

2 Listen. Choose Michael **or** Lin and match the words with them.

A 3

Höre zu. Wähle Michael **oder** Lin und ordne ihnen die Wörter zu.

Russia ✓ | China | be successful | better life | achieve dreams | happy family, health, enough money | family | friends

Culture
New York City hat weltweit die größte jüdische Bevölkerung.

A

Michael

B

Lin

	Michael	Lin
Family is from:	*Russia*	*C*
Their American Dream:		
A successful life for them:		
What makes him/her happy:		

✓ Ich kann ein Interview verstehen.

Finding a new home

A 4

A

North Hotel
5th Avenue
New York City
USA

18th January 1898

My dear Mary,
New York is a noisy city with lots of people. I arrived at Ellis Island two weeks ago with people from lots of other countries. We were all very tired, and I wished I was back in London with you.
I am feeling much better now. I work at the North Hotel in the kitchen. The chef is loud and often angry, but he is fair. I share a small room in the hotel with two other men who work at the hotel. They are good men.
I hope you are well. I am counting the weeks until you are here.
I feel sure we will have a wonderful future in this new country.
With lots of love,
Albert

A 5

B

28th May 1898

I have been at sea for almost three weeks now, and there is still no sign of America. Food and water are never enough, and we are always hungry.
I share a cabin with seven other women and girls. There is no fresh air, and we share one toilet between 16 people. I miss Albert so much.
It is another four days until I will see him again!

A 6

C

WHITE STAR LINE

LIVERPOOL – QUEENSTOWN – NEW YORK CITY

Passenger ticket No. 458977

Date: 9th May 1898

Name	*Mary Backshall*	Age	*23*
From	*Liverpool*	To	*NYC*
Class	*Third Class*	Cabin	*25F*

1 Read the texts. Lies die Texte.

2 Match the texts with the types of texts.

Verbinde die Texte mit den Textsorten.

A ticket

B letter

C diary entry

Jede Textsorte hat ihre eigenen Merkmale. Worin unterscheidet sich z. B. ein Brief von einem Tagebucheintrag?

3 Finding a new home

a) Complete the text about Albert and Mary.

Vervollständige den Text über Albert und Mary.

four | hotel | ship | 1898 ✓ | New York City | cabin | wonderful future

In January 1898 ______ Albert wrote a letter to Mary. He was in ______ then. He worked in the kitchen of a ______.

Albert and Mary wanted to have a ______ in the USA.

Mary wrote a diary entry in May 1898. She was on a ______ then.

She wrote about the food and her ______. Life was not good on the ship. She arrived in New York city ______ days later.

b) Answer the questions about the ticket.

Beantworte die Fragen zum Ticket.

1. Whose ticket is it? It's Mary Backshall's ______ ticket.
2. How old is she? She's ______ years old.
3. What is her cabin number? It's cabin ______.
4. When did the ship leave? It left on ______.
5. Where did the ship start? It started in ______.

✓ Ich kann verschiedene Texte zu einem Thema verstehen.

Checklist

Complete Sophia's answers.

Vervollständige Sophias Antworten.

took the subway | stayed in a hotel | was fantastic ✓
ate lots of pizzas | stayed for four days | was Central Park

You Hi Sophia. How was your trip to New York?

Sophia Hi. The trip *was fantastic* ________.

You Where did you stay?

Sophia My friend Nathan and I ________ ________ near the Hudson River.

You What did you see in New York?

Sophia We saw lots of famous places. My favourite place ________.

You Did you take the bus to get around the city?

Sophia No, we didn't. We walked or ________ ________.

You What did you eat?

Sophia We ________. The Italian restaurants in New York are great.

You How long did you stay in New York?

Sophia We ________. We'll be back next year.

A

B

C

D

E

F

Task: A presentation

Give a presentation about a person who has been successful.
Präsentiere eine Person, die erfolgreich war oder ist.

Step 1: Choose a successful person. This can be a famous person or someone you know.
Suche dir eine erfolgreiche Person aus. Das kann jemand Berühmtes sein oder jemand, den oder die du kennst.

Examples:
Alice Augusta Ball (scientist), Sümeyye Boyac (Paralympic swimmer), Ryyan Alshebl (first Syrian mayor of a German town), …

Step 2: Find out more about this person online. Take notes on what makes them successful.
Finde online mehr über die Person heraus. Mache dir Notizen dazu, was sie erfolgreich macht.

Alice Augusta Ball
- *born in 1892*
- *lived in Hawaii*
- *first African American who finished College of Hawaii*
- *first woman who taught chemistry there*
- *…*

Step 3: Make a draft. Introduce the person and say what's special about them.
Schreibe einen Entwurf.
Stelle die Person vor und sage, was das Besondere an ihr ist.

Alice Augusta Ball was a scientist. She was born in 1892 and lived in Hawaii. She was the first African American who finished College of Hawaii. Ball was also the first woman who taught chemistry there. …

Step 4: Add one or more photos.
Füge ein oder mehrere Fotos hinzu.

Step 5: Practise the presentation.
Übe die Präsentation.

The Northeast – past and present

Native Americans had lived in the Northeast for thousands of years when the first European settlers arrived and founded colonies. By 1776 there were 13 colonies, which became the first states of the USA.

1 Read the texts about the Northeast.

Lies die Texte über den Nordosten.

1

1 Before 1600 **the Patuxet** Native Americans lived in the Northeast. But 20 years later European diseases[1] had killed almost all the Patuxet. Today visitors can learn about them at the Plimoth Patuxet Museums.

1 disease – *die Krankheit*

2 The ship **the Mayflower** came to America from Plymouth in England in 1620. There were 102 passengers on it. They founded New Plymouth, the first permanent[2] colony in America. They were later called 'Pilgrims'.

2 permanent – *dauerhaft*

2

3 Boston was an important city in 1773. In that year there was a protest against British taxes[3] on tea. The people threw tea into the sea there. This protest is called the 'Boston Tea Party'.
Today Boston is a center for artificial intelligence[4] and biotechnology[5].

3 tax – *die Steuer*
4 artificial intelligence – *die künstliche Intelligenz*
5 biotechnology – *die Biotechnologie*

4 On July 4, 1776, people from the 13 colonies signed[6] **the Declaration of Independence** in Philadelphia. The flag of the USA has 13 stripes[7] for the first 13 colonies and 50 stars for the 50 states of the USA today.

6 to sign – *unterschreiben*
7 stripe – *der Streifen*

2 What did you already know? What did you find interesting?

Was wusstest du schon? Was fandest du interessant?

about the Boston Tea Party | that many Native Americans died | ...
people threw tea into the water | ...
people from the Mayflower are called 'Pilgrims' now | ...

I already knew about the Declaration of Independence.

I didn't know that the American flag shows the colonies and states.

It's interesting that European diseases killed Native Americans.

The Northeast in pictures

1 Complete the names. Vervollständige die Namen.

White | space | Mount | Hudson | Fifth ✓ | Niagara | Liberty | Island | whale

A

F I F T H
Avenue

B

_ _ _ _ _ _ _
Falls

C

Ellis
_ _ _ _ _ _

D

_ _ _ _ _
Washington

E

Statue of
_ _ _ _ _ _ _

F

_ _ _ _ _
House

G

_ _ _ _ _
shuttle

H

_ _ _ _ _
watching

I

_ _ _ _ _ _
River

2 Complete the sentence with the letters from the grey boxes.
Vervollständige den Satz mit den Buchstaben aus den grauen Kästchen.

America's flag is called the

S T _ _ _ and S _ _ _ _ _ _ .

Unit quiz

1 Tick the right information.

Setze ein Häkchen bei den richtigen Informationen.

1. The biggest city in the Northeast is …
   - **I** ☑ New York.
   - **P** ☐ Philadelphia.
2. About 8 million people live in …
   - **O** ☐ Washington.
   - **A** ☐ New York.
3. The name 'New York' came from …
   - **F** ☐ tourists.
   - **G** ☐ English settlers.
4. The Northeast coast is great for …
   - **T** ☐ kayaking.
   - **A** ☐ whale watching.
5. You can watch whales there …
   - **R** ☐ from May to October.
   - **B** ☐ in April.
6. The highest point in the Northeast is …
   - **A** ☐ Mount Washington.
   - **R** ☐ Lake Eerie.
7. How much of the US economy is in the Northeast?
   - **A** ☐ 23 %
   - **K** ☐ 30 %
8. When did the attack on the World Trade Center happen?
   - **E** ☐ 11th September (9/11) 2011
   - **L** ☐ 11th September (9/11) 2001
9. Success is part of the …
   - **M** ☐ Northeast farms.
   - **L** ☐ American dream.
10. The Northeast is very …
    - **N** ☐ poor.
    - **S** ☐ rich.

2 Complete the sentence with the right letters from exercise 1.

Vervollständige den Satz mit den richtigen Buchstaben aus Aufgabe 1.

A beautiful sight in the Northeast:

N [I] [ ] [ ] [ ] [ ] [ ] F [ ] [ ] [ ] [ ].

2 Off to the Midwest

In dieser Unit wirst du …
- etwas über den Mittleren Westen erfahren.
- über das Schulleben sprechen.
- eine Radiosendung anhören.
- über Feiertage und Feste sprechen.
- eine Live-Doku anschauen.
- einen Ausschnitt aus einer Kurzgeschichte lesen.

A

B

This is the USA's most important farming region. It has large corn and soy fields. There are car factories too.

INFO

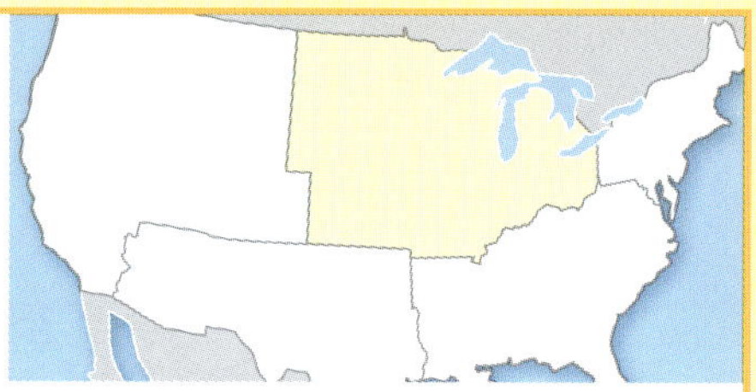

Sights: Mount Rushmore, the Great Lakes, Badlands National Park
Time zones: three

C

The Oglala Nation live in South Dakota. In the past they hunted bison. Visitors can learn about them at a museum.

D

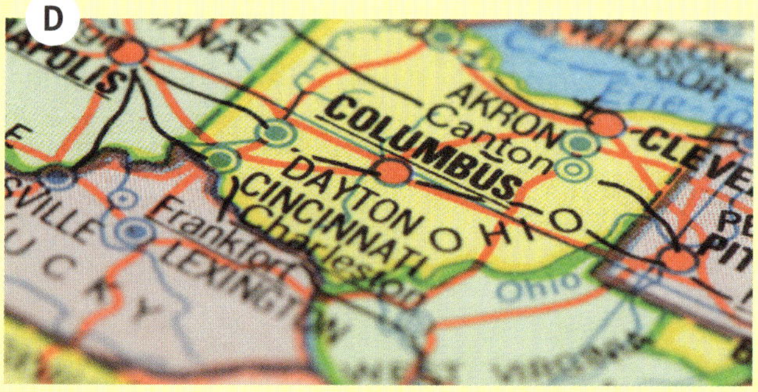

Many Germans came to the Midwest in the 19th century. Some towns here have names like Dresden.

E

The Kansas City Chiefs are a football team who have won the Super Bowl four times.

F

Al Capone was a famous criminal in Chicago in the 1920s. There are many movies about his life.

1 Facts about the Midwest

a) Read the texts. Add the words to the mind map.
Lies die Texte. Ergänze die Wörter auf der Mindmap.

Al Capone | the Oglala Nation | Super Bowl winners | farming | Germans | large fields ✓ | cars

Zwei Linien beschreibst du erst in Aufgabe b).

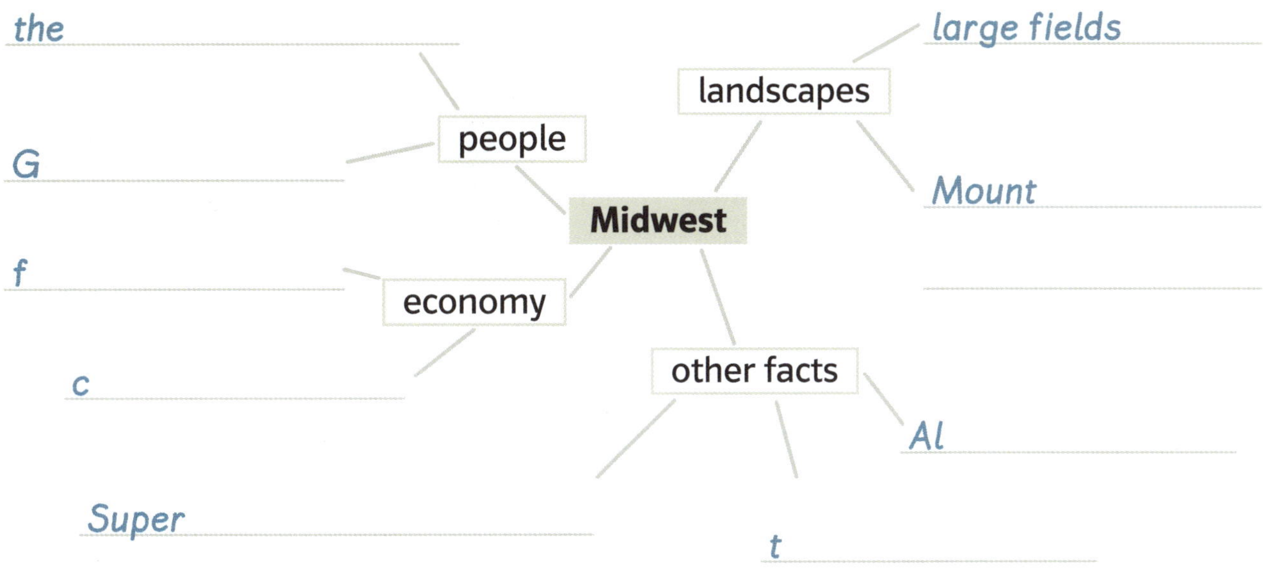

b) Watch the film. Tick the right answers and add them to the mind map in a). Schau dir den Film an. Setze Häkchen bei den richtigen Antworten und ergänze sie in der Mindmap in a).

V 4

1. You can see four presidents on
   - ☐ the Rocky Mountains.
   - ☐ Mount Rushmore.

2. Sometimes there are
   - ☐ fires
   - ☐ tornadoes.

c) Talk about the Midwest. Sprich über den Mittleren Westen.

The Midwest is famous for car factories. | farming | Mount Rushmore | …

In the past many Germans lived there. | the Oglala hunted bison | …

I think it's interesting that the Kansas City Chiefs are so successful. | there are three time zones there | cities have German names | …

✓ Ich kann Informationen über den Mittleren Westen verstehen.

High school life

1 Read the blog. Lies den Blog. ► Vokabeln S. 124 (V3)

Internet

11/05/2024

Hey, it's Lena, welcome to my blog! I'm an exchange student at a high school in Columbus, Ohio. I started school here in September. Find out what it's really like!

I get up at 6:30. There's a dress code at school: Students aren't allowed to wear short tops, for example! Me and my host sister Paisley meet our friends where the yellow school bus stops and ride to school together.

At school we have to walk through a metal detector. That felt strange at first! And if you're late three times, you have to go to detention.

We start the day with homeroom at 8:00. Our teacher gives us information and news about school events, and we can talk if we have any problems. Students also take the Pledge of Allegiance every day.

Everyone has subjects like math and English. But there are also classes we can choose, for example, film production and drama. How cool is that?

There are clubs after school every day, so I stay there longer than in Germany. I go to a foreign language club and the yearbook club. Paisley is a member of the student council. We all watch an American football game at school on Friday afternoons. It's an amazing event.

I'm loving it here. If you have any questions, please post them! Bye!

2 Complete the sentences. Vervollständige die Sätze.

American football | September ✓ | choose | dress code | clubs | bus

1. Lena started school in the USA in *September* .
2. The high school has a ______ .
3. Lena and Paisley go to school by ______ .
4. Students can ______ some of their subjects.
5. Lena stays at school longer to go to different ______ .
6. Students watch an ______ game every Friday.

3 What did you find most interesting about the blog?

Was fandet ihr am interessantesten am Blog?

walk through a metal detector | can't wear short tops | take the Pledge of Allegiance every day | …

A I found most interesting that students can choose some subjects .

B I was surprised that … .

4 Match the definitions with the words.

Ordne den Definitionen die Wörter zu.

1. rules about what you can wear — dress code
2. a device that beeps when it is close to metal
3. when a student has broken the rules and must stay longer
4. where students get information
5. a book with pictures and information about all students
6. students who plan things for other students

detention
homeroom
dress code
metal detector
student council
yearbook

5 Mediation: Answer the questions in German.

Sprachmittlung: Beantworte die Fragen auf Deutsch.

Hey guys, I'm Olivia, your president. I want to start health days with yoga and healthy cooking classes.

Hey everyone, I'm Grant, your vice president. I'm going to organize the spring festival this year.

Hi, I'm Nolan. I'm the secretary this year. I organize meetings.

Hello, I'm Laura, and I'm the treasurer. I help decide how much money each club gets.

1. Wie viele Mitglieder hat die Schülervertretung? – *vier* ______
2. Welche vier Rollen gibt es? – ______
3. Um welche vier Aufgaben kümmern die Mitglieder sich? – ______

6 Read Lena's blog again. Compare her school with your own. Complete the sentences.

Lies Lenas Blog nochmal. Vergleiche ihre Schule mit deiner eigenen. Vervollständige die Sätze.

Lena's school has a *dress code* ______. Our school ______. Subjects are different too. Lena can choose subjects like ______ ______. We ______ ______ at our school.

Schreibe auf die grünen Linien, wie es an Lenas Schule in den USA ist. Auf die blauen schreibst du, wie es bei dir ist.

Language

Tut jemand etwas regelmäßig, kommt bei **he**, **she** und **it** ein **s** zum Verb:

The bus leave**s** at 7:25. Lena **doesn't** wear short tops.

7 Complete the sentences. Vervollständige die Sätze.

isn't | organises | choose

1. Camilla and I always ______________ the same subjects.
2. The gym ______________ open on Mondays.
3. Nolan ______________ meetings.

8 Complete the sentences. Vervollständige die Sätze.

writes | don't do | talks ✓ | cook | doesn't play | hang out

A

Lena *talks* to her parents every Sunday.

B

She and Paisley ______________ on Saturdays.

C

Her host parents sometimes ______________.

D

Lena and Paisley ______________ their homework together.

E

Lena ______________ ______________ lacrosse at school.

F

She often ______________ her blog in the evenings.

9 **Your turn:** A leaflet about your school

Make a leaflet for new students from other countries.

Macht eine Broschüre für neue Schülerinnen und Schüler aus anderen Ländern.

Step 1: Get into groups. Think about important topics for school life.
Bildet Gruppen. Überlegt euch wichtige Themen fürs Schulleben.

- *subjects*
- *sports*
- *food and drink*
- ...

Step 2: Collect information that a new student would need to know. You can search the school's website or ask a teacher.
Sammelt Informationen, die ein neuer Schüler oder eine neue Schülerin wissen muss. Ihr könnt auf der Internetseite eurer Schule suchen oder eine Lehrkraft fragen.

Things to know	Examples, when, where, who
subjects	– *must take: ...* – *choose: ...*
sports	– *basketball (Friday, 2 p.m., in the gym)* – ...
...	...

Step 3: Structure you notes.
Ordnet eure Notizen.

1. *subjects*
2. *sports*
3. ...

Step 4: Write short texts.
Schreibt kurze Texte.

Sports
Our school has .... You can ....
It's open ....

Step 5: Add photos.
Fügt Fotos hinzu.

The school gym

Step 6: Organise all your texts and photos and make your leaflet.
Organisiert eure Texte und Fotos und erstellt euren Flyer.

✓ Ich kann über das Schulleben sprechen.

Meet the farmers

1 Match the words with the photos. Ordne die Begriffe den Bildern zu.

dairy | cherries | costs | acres ✓ | grass | to produce

A

acres

B

C

D

E

F

2 Listen to the radio show. Tick the right information.

A 7

Höre dir die Radiosendung an. Setze Häkchen bei den richtigen Informationen.

1. Fischer's farm produces	☐ corn.	☑ milk.
2. One of their problems are	☐ high energy costs.	☐ ill cows.
3. They also produce	☐ ice cream & yoghurt.	☐ coffee.
4. Allen's farm is about 1,200	☐ miles long.	☐ acres.
5. They have	☐ twelve workers.	☐ ten workers.
6. They are opening a small hotel	☐ in three years.	☐ next year.

✓ Ich kann eine Radiosendung verstehen.

Happy holidays

1 Read the dialogue. Lies dir das Gespräch durch.

It's Thanksgiving morning, and Brad is at home with his parents and his younger brother Lincoln in Cincinnati, Ohio. Brad is making a video call to his sister Regan. She's in Austin, Texas.

Regan Hey Brad, what's happening at home?
Brad Hey Regan, we're all busy here! Dad's preparing the turkey and Mom's making the pumpkin pie.
Regan OK! What's Lincoln doing?
Brad He's cleaning the living room now.
Regan Great! What else will we have for Thanksgiving dinner?
Brad Grandpa has made cornbread, and Grandma has made pecan pie. You love that, don't you?
Regan Yes, I can't wait! So, what are you doing to help?
Brad I'm making my Thanksgiving fruit punch!
Regan That's cool!
Brad What time is your flight?
Regan I should be in Cincinnati at about 6 o'clock your time.
Brad Mom and I will pick you up at the airport. I have to make that punch now. See you later!
Regan That's awesome. Thank you! See you later!

Culture
„Thanksgiving" ist einer der wichtigsten Feiertage in den USA. Er wird am vierten Donnerstag im November gefeiert. Es gibt ein großes Essen mit Truthahn, Kürbiskuchen und mehr. Die Leute erzählen sich oft gegenseitig, wofür sie dankbar sind.

2 Answer the questions. Beantworte die Fragen.

Brad and their mum. | Austin, Texas. | by plane. | pecan pie.

1. Where is Regan? She's in ______
2. What food does Regan love? She loves ______
3. How will Regan travel later? She will travel ______
4. Who will meet her at the airport? ______

3 Match the photos with the right phrases. ► Vokabeln S. 125 (V4)

Ordne die Fotos den richtigen Wendungen zu.

A

B

C

D

E

F

1. to give or receive presents [C]
2. to put up decorations [ ]
3. to watch or take part in a parade [ ]
4. to wear special clothes [ ]
5. to light candles [ ]
6. to prepare and eat a special meal [ ]

4 Talk about the activities in exercise 3.

Sprecht über die Aktivitäten in Aufgabe 3.

A At Christmas we usually light candles.

B That's cool! I always put up decorations on my birthday.

5 Listen and put the sentences in the right order.

A 8

Höre zu und bringe die Sätze in die richtige Reihenfolge.

A Regan's flight has been delayed by an hour. ☐

B Regan's friend is going to stay in Austin. 1

C Regan is still waiting for her bag. ☐

D She will arrive in Cincinnati at about 8 p.m. ☐

Culture

Die USA sind ein sehr großes Land mit verschiedenen Zeitzonen. Es kann also sein, dass du die Zeit umstellen musst, wenn du von einem Staat in einen anderen reist.

6 Choose the right answers.

Wähle die richtigen Antworten aus.

1. What is in the cartoon?
   - ☐ There's a chicken and a girl.
   - ☑ There's a turkey and a woman.
2. Where are they?
   - ☐ They're in a travel agency.
   - ☐ They're on holiday.
3. Who says the sentence and why?
   - ☐ It's the woman. She wants to go to a warmer place.
   - ☐ It's the turkey. It's afraid that people will eat it at Thanksgiving.

"I'd like to spend November and December in a foreign country."

Skills

In Cartoons ist die Kultur eines Landes oft sehr wichtig. Um einen Cartoon über Thanksgiving in den USA zu verstehen, muss man z. B. wissen, dass das Fest im November stattfindet und dass traditionell Truthahn gegessen wird.

Language
Wenn etwas gerade jetzt passiert, verwendest du **am**, **is** oder **are** und hängst **ing** ans Ende des Verbs:

I'**m** wait**ing** at the moment.
He **isn't** help**ing** right now.
Are you mak**ing** punch?

Fragewörter kommen noch vor **am**, **is** oder **are**: "**Why** is it raining so hard?"

7 Complete the phone call. Vervollständige das Telefongespräch.

are staying | are having ✓ | is winning | am playing | isn't playing

Alice Hi Regan. How's Thanksgiving?

Regan Hi. We *are having* ______ a lot of fun. I ______ a game with Brad and Moira at the moment. How about you?

Alice We ______ with Pedro's parents. It's cold here!

Brad Hey Regan, come back! Moira ______ the game!

Regan OK, I have to go. Would you like to speak to Mom? She ______.

Alice Sure, speak soon Regan!

8 Make sentences. Bilde Sätze.

1. cool costumes. | are wearing | The people

   The people are ______

2. in the parade | The carnival king | in this photo. | is riding

   ______

3. These people | in the Fire & Ice Run. | are taking part

   ______

9 **Your turn:** A slide show

Present a slideshow with photos from a special event.

Präsentiere eine Slideshow mit Fotos von einem besonderen Ereignis.

Step 1: Think of a celebration or other event that you enjoyed.
Denke an eine Feier oder ein anderes Ereignis, das dir Spaß gemacht hat.

Step 2: Search for photos of the event.
Suche nach Bildern von dem Ereignis.

S Skills
Denke daran, die abgebildeten Personen zu fragen, ehe du anderen ein Foto von ihnen zeigst.

Step 3: Choose five to ten photos. Organise them in a presentation tool.
Suche dir fünf bis zehn Fotos aus. Organisiere sie in einer Präsentationssoftware.

Step 4: Write a short introduction: Which day or event? Who? Where? When?
Schreibe eine kurze Einleitung: Welcher Tag oder welches Event? Wer? Wo? Wann?

My cousin's birthday
- *my cousin's family and 20 guests*
- *at my cousin's house*
- *after breakfast, 4th April*

Step 5: Write about the photos. Use the present progressive.
Schreibe etwas zu den Fotos. Verwende das present progressive.

In this photo you can see my cousin. She is eating a piece of cake. My mum is dancing with my grandpa. ...

Step 6: Present the slideshow.
Präsentiere die Slideshow.

✓ Ich kann über Feiertage und Feste sprechen.

Storm chasers

V 5

1 Watch the film. Talk about how it makes you feel. Schaut euch den Film an. Sprecht darüber, wie ihr euch beim Ansehen fühlt.

Media tip
Durch bestimmte Kamera-einstellungen und die Musik kann ein Film z. B. traurig oder aufregend wirken.

A The film makes me feel afraid.   excited   sad   …

B I think what the film shows looks exciting.   dangerous   fascinating   …

A

B

V 5

2 Watch the film again. Complete the sentences.
Schau dir den Film nochmal an. Vervollständige die Sätze.

shut   violent   channel   chase ✓

1. Reed and his team *chase* (jagen) the storm in a car.
2. They have to ______ (schließen) the windows .
3. Reed calls a local weather ______ (Sender).
4. The tornado is very ______ (brutal).

3 Talk to a partner. Would you like to be a storm chaser?
Unterhaltet euch. Wärt ihr gerne Sturmjäger?

A I'd like to be a storm chaser because I'd like to have an exciting job.   work in a team   be a hero   …

B I wouldn't like to be a storm chaser because I don't want to get hurt.   it's dangerous   it's scary   …

✓ Ich kann eine Live-Doku verstehen.

Fancy dancer by Monique Gray Smith

1 Talk about the pictures. What do you think the story is about?
Sprecht über die Bilder. Was glaubt ihr, worum es geht?

A I think it could be about a family argument.
B I think the story could be about magic.

a celebration | a boy | a car ride | …

2 Read the text. Lies den Text.

A 9

Rory is eleven years old and lives in Ann Arbor, Michigan, USA. His mother is a Cree Native American from Canada.
He has a little sister, Suzie.
This is the first part of a longer story.

S Skills
Du musst nicht alle Wörter kennen, um die Geschichte zu verstehen. Wichtige Wörter kannst du nachschlagen.

My father left when I was nine. One day, he just never came home. It was hard to see how much Suzie missed him. But I was happy. You see, my father was not a nice man. Not to me, my sister, or my mom.

I'm sure he hated that my mom was Cree. Why else wouldn't he let her speak Cree in our house, or do anything that was part of our culture?

I remember my mom celebrating her culture once. I was about seven or eight. It was the middle of the night, and I was thirsty, so I went to the kitchen for a drink. I saw a light and heard music. The music was new to me, but it was powerful. There was my mom, dancing. She stood with her head high and her feet quietly moved to the drum. In her hand was what looked like feathers.

That night I learned that my mom was much stronger than I'd thought.

I'm sure my father was ashamed of us. He often told Suzie and me that we'd have a better life if we looked more Irish, like him. I knew Mom was proud of me, and that was all I needed. Until she brought Paul home.

Paul is Cree like us. Not long after he came into our lives, Mom contacted her family again. Although we couldn't go to Canada to meet them, we were talking online two or three times a week. I was part of a big family. I looked like them. I really loved watching how Mom laughed.

A 10

A few months after Paul came to live with us, we were in the car when he turned on some music. It was the same music Mom listened to that night I saw her dancing in the kitchen. My head began to move to the music.

"You ever been to a powwow?" Paul asked.

"What's a powwow?" I asked him.

"One of the greatest events ever. We dance, sing, visit people, and laugh." Paul smiled, "But really, powwow is a way of celebrating our traditions, our families, and our ancestors."

"Is it just us?" I asked. "You know, uh, Native Americans?"

"Mostly, yes. Native people from all over the country go to powwows, but non-Natives are welcome too. That's part of what makes the powwow beautiful, the sharing of cultures. I think you could be a fancy dancer."

"OK, first, I don't know what a fancy dancer is. And second …"

I remembered my father's voice. *You sure ain't got any hopes of being on any sports team.*

"I'm not good at sports. I think I'd suck[1] as a fancy dancer."

Paul started talking again. "Your mom told me how your dad treated you. How he treated all of you. I'm sorry that happened. I understand why you think you wouldn't be a good fancy dancer. But people who aren't good at sports can dance too. You can dance to tell a story to the music."

Paul was quiet until we arrived at our house. "There is a lot of strength in your heart, Rory. You can let the awful things your father said define you. Or –"

"Or what?" I asked.

1 to suck – *total schlecht sein (umgangssprachlich)*

3 Talk about the story. Do you like it?

Sprecht über die Geschichte. Gefällt sie euch?

A I like the story. I think it's beautiful because Paul helps Rory.

nice | interesting | ...

it's about powwows | ...

B I don't like the story. I felt sad when I read that Suzie missed her father.

angry | bored | ...

about the father | ...

4 Circle the right words. Kreise die richtigen Wörter ein.

1. Rory's father left when Rory was **five** | **nine**.
2. Rory saw his mother dancing one **night** | **day**.
3. After she met Paul, Rory's mother contacted her family in **New York** | **Canada**.
4. Rory listens to **Native American** | **pop** music in Paul's car.
5. Paul says that Rory can be a **basketball player** | **fancy dancer**.

Skills

Bei Geschichten in der Ich-Form kann die erzählende Person sagen, was sie denkt und wie sie sich fühlt. Wir erfahren nur ihre Sicht auf die Dinge.

5 Are the sentences true or false? Tick.

Sind die Sätze wahr oder falsch? Setze Häkchen.

	true	false
1. Rory's father likes Cree culture.	☐	☐
2. When Rory saw his mother dancing, he thought that she was strong.	☐	☐
3. Rory's mother felt happy when she contacted her family.	☐	☐
4. Rory likes Paul more than his father.	☐	☐
5. Rory thinks that he can be a good dancer.	☐	☐

6 The power of words

a) Tick the sentence with the same meaning.

Setze ein Häkchen bei dem Satz mit derselben Bedeutung.

Rory's father:

"You sure ain't got any hope of being on any sports team."

A You'll never be good at it. ☐

B I was better when I was you age. ☐

b) Choose an ending for Paul's sentence or write one of your own.

Such dir ein Ende für Paul's Satz aus oder schreibe dein eigenes.

"You can let the awful things your father said define you. Or — "

… you can live your own life. ☐

… you can try new things. ☐

… you can follow your dreams. ☐

… ....

7 Make freeze frames of the family's life with the father and with Paul.

Erstellt Standbilder zum Familienleben mit dem Vater und mit Paul.

1. Sucht euch zwei Szenen aus dem Text aus.
2. Entscheidet euch, wer wen in welcher Szene darstellen soll.
3. Sprecht darüber, welche Gefühle die Figuren füreinander haben und wie sich die Situation geändert hat.
4. Benutzt Körpersprache um eure Gefühle auszudrücken. Ihr könnt zum Beispiel die Arme verschränken, auf den Boden schauen, die Schultern hängen lassen, oder ihr könnt lächeln, jemanden freundlich ansehen, … .
5. Stellt eure Standbilder der Klasse vor.

✓ Ich kann einen Ausschnitt aus einer Kurzgeschichte verstehen.

Checklist

Look at the photos and complete the video call.

Schau dir die Fotos an und vervollständige den Videoanruf.

pecan pie | fruit punch | cornbread | turkey ✓ | parade

Brad Hi Leon. What's happening at your house?

Leon Hi Brad. Everybody is busy. Guess what? My sister's preparing the *turkey* this year.

Brad Great. What are you doing?

Leon I'd like to make a ______________ like yours. Can I have your recipe, please?

Brad Yes, of course. Have your grandparents already arrived? My grandma has made her famous ______________. I love it.

Leon My grandparents arrived yesterday. Grandpa is making ______________. What is Lincoln doing?

Brad Lincoln is watching the ______________ on TV. I'll send you my punch recipe now. Then I have to make the punch for us.

Leon Thank you, bye.

Brad Bye!

A

B

C

D

E

Task: Thanksgiving in class

Prepare a Thanksgiving celebration in your class.

Bereitet ein Thanksgiving Fest in eurer Klasse vor.

Step 1: Collect words for Thanksgiving dishes.
Sammelt Wörter für Thanksgiving-Gerichte.

turkey sandwiches
Thanksgiving
cornbread
...

Step 2: Decide which dishes you want to prepare.
Entscheidet, welche Gerichte ihr zubereiten wollt.
Answer these questions:

- Does anyone have **allergies**?
- Is anyone a **vegetarian** or **vegan**? Does anyone **not eat** certain foods?
- Are the dishes **easy** to make?

Skills
Ihr könnt diese Ausdrücke benutzen:
... is allergic to ... .
... can't eat ... .
... doesn't/don't eat ... .
That's an easy/difficult dish.

Step 3: Get into groups. Decide who makes which dish.
Bildet Gruppen. Entscheidet, wer welches Gericht macht.

Ayshe, Tim, Sara, Mohamed: turkey sandwiches
Leon, Anita, ...

Step 4: Find a recipe for your dish.
Findet ein Rezept für euer Gericht.

Media tip
Ihr könnt im Internet Filme anschauen, wie man bestimmte Gerichte zubereitet.

Step 5: Meet to prepare your dish or dishes. Then bring them to class.
Trefft euch, um euer Gericht zuzubereiten. Dann bringt es zum Unterricht.

The Great Lakes

1 Which famous lakes do you already know? What can you do there?
Welche berühmten Seen kennst du bereits? Was kannst du dort machen?

1

1 The Lakes

The five Great Lakes are Superior, Michigan, Huron, Erie, and Ontario. They are the largest group of freshwater[1] lakes in the world. Part of the border[2] between the USA and Canada runs through the Great Lakes.

1 freshwater – *das Süßwasser*
2 border – *die Grenze*

2 Water of life

21% of the world's freshwater is in the Great Lakes. Over 30 million people get freshwater from the lakes. They also water[3] forests and farms across the Midwest and much of Canada.

3 to water – *bewässern*

2

3

3 Wild animals

There are a lot of beautiful wild animals in the Great Lakes region. Many kinds of fish swim in the Lakes. They are also home to otters[4] and beavers[5]. Gray wolves and moose[6] live near the lakes too.

4 otter – *der Otter*
5 beaver – *der Bieber*
6 moose – *der Elch, die Elche*

4 Shipwrecks[7]

The weather on the Lakes often changes quickly. This can make it dangerous for ships. People say more than 6,000 ships have sunk[8] there. The lakes are so deep[9] that we don't know where all the ships are.

7 shipwreck – *das Schiffswrack*
8 sunk – *gesunken*
9 deep – *tief*

4

2 What surprised you? What would you like to learn more about?

Was hat dich überrascht? Worüber würdest du gerne mehr lernen?

there are shipwrecks in the Lakes | those animals live in the USA | …
farmers and forests need the Lakes | the USA have so much water | …
the weather on the Lakes | animals in the USA | …

I was surprised that ______________________________.

I didn't know that ______________________________.

I'd like to learn more about ______________________________.

Unit quiz

Die richtigen Antworten findest du auf den Seiten, die hinter den Sätzen stehen.

1 Facts about the Midwest

a) True or false? Tick.
Richtig oder falsch? Setze Häkchen.

	true	false
1. The Midwest is most important for fishing. ► p.30	☐	☐
2. The Kansas City Chiefs are policemen. ► p.30	☐	☐
3. Very few Germans came in the 19th century. ► p.30	☐	☐
4. They gave their children names like Dresden. ► p.30	☐	☐
5. Students walk through a metal detector at school. ► p.32	☐	☐
6. Tornadoes are very violent storms. ► p.43	☐	☐
7. The five Great Lakes are the largest group of freshwater in the world. ► p.50	☐	☐
8. Over 30 million people get fresh fish from the lakes. ► p.50	☐	☐

b) Correct the wrong facts. Write full sentences.
Korrigiere die falschen Angaben. Schreibe ganze Sätze.

a football team | freshwater | farming ✓ | Many | towns

1. *The Midwest is most important for farming.*
2. ______________________________
3. ______________________________
4. ______________________________
5. ______________________________

School life in Columbus, Ohio

1 Circle the right answers and do the crossword.

Kreise die richtigen Antworten ein und löse das Kreuzworträtsel.

1. High school in Columbus, Ohio, starts in **August** | **September**.
2. Everyone has to walk through a metal detector at **the bus stop** | **school**.
3. If students are late, they have to go to **detention** | **the director**.
4. The school day starts at 8:00 with **homeroom** | **detention**.
5. You get news there and you can talk about **friends** | **problems**.
6. There are clubs after school every **Friday** | **day**.
7. You can go to a foreign **language** | **sports** club, for example.
8. **German** | **American** football is a popular club at American schools.

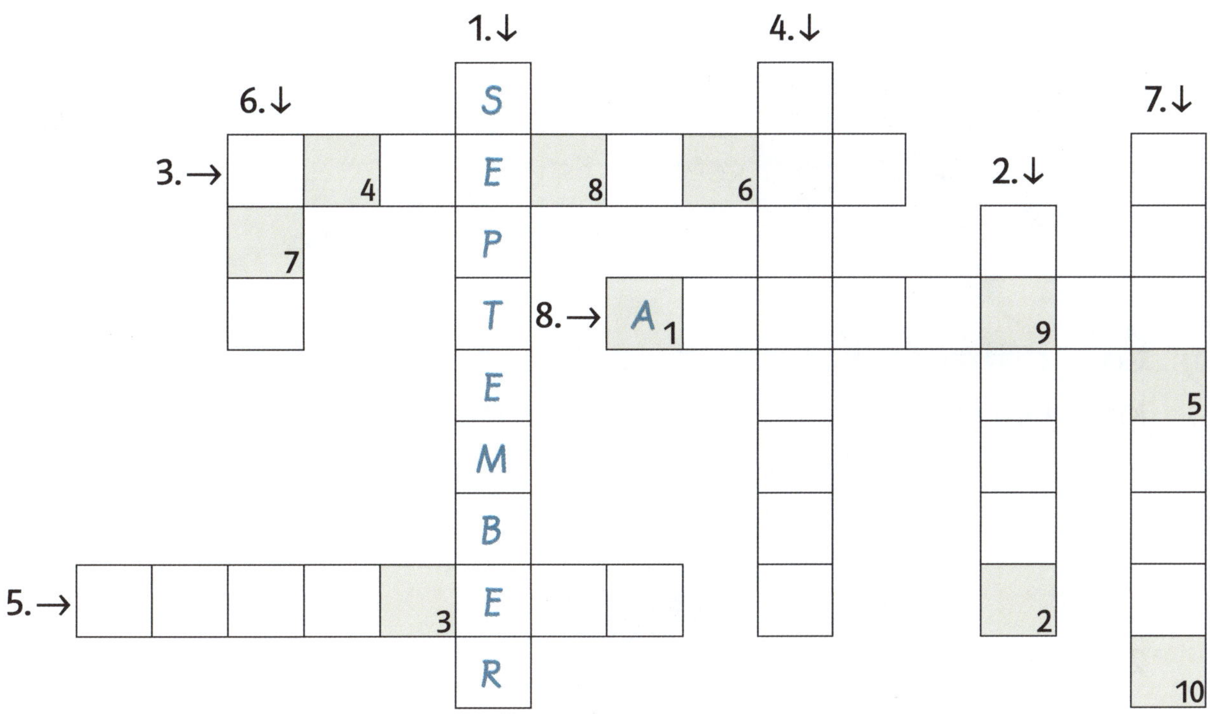

2 Complete the sentence with the letters from the grey boxes.

Vervollständige den Satz mit den Buchstaben aus den grauen Kästchen.

American students take the Pledge of

1	2	3	4	5	6	7	8	9	10
A									

every day.

3 Going to the West

In dieser Unit wirst du …
- etwas über den Westen erfahren.
- über den Lebenszyklus eines Produkts sprechen.
- eine Reportage anschauen.
- ein soziales Projekt vorstellen.
- ein Hörspiel anhören.
- einen Zeitschriftenartikel lesen.

A

B

The volcanoes of Hawaii and the deserts of Nevada are fantastic landscapes. Surfing is very popular.

INFO

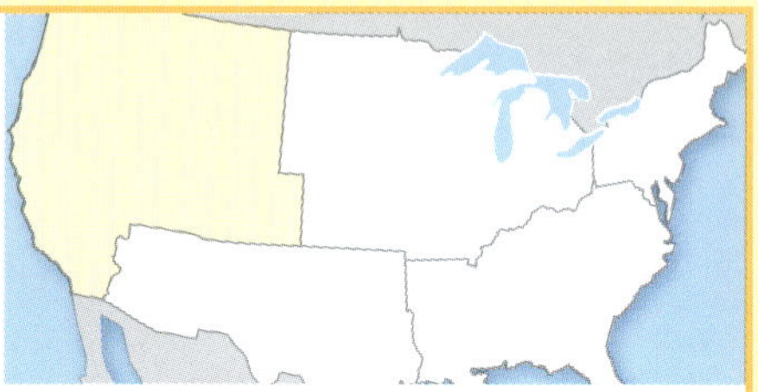

Sights: Golden Gate Bridge
Hottest place: Death Valley, California, 57°C

C

Many people of Hispanic or Asian background live in California. Spanish is the second language there.

D

The biggest internet, social media, and entertainment platforms are in Silicon Valley.

E

The West produces the most fruit in the USA. Many people work on fruit farms there.

F

Some places in the West have to save water, and there are also wildfires in California and other states.

1 Facts about the West

a) Read the texts. Add the words to the mind map.
Lies die Texte. Ergänze die Wörter in der Mindmap.

Die zwei leeren Lücken füllst du in Aufgabe b) aus.

fruit farms | Hispanics and Asians | Silicon Valley | forests ✓ | deserts | volcanoes | wildfires

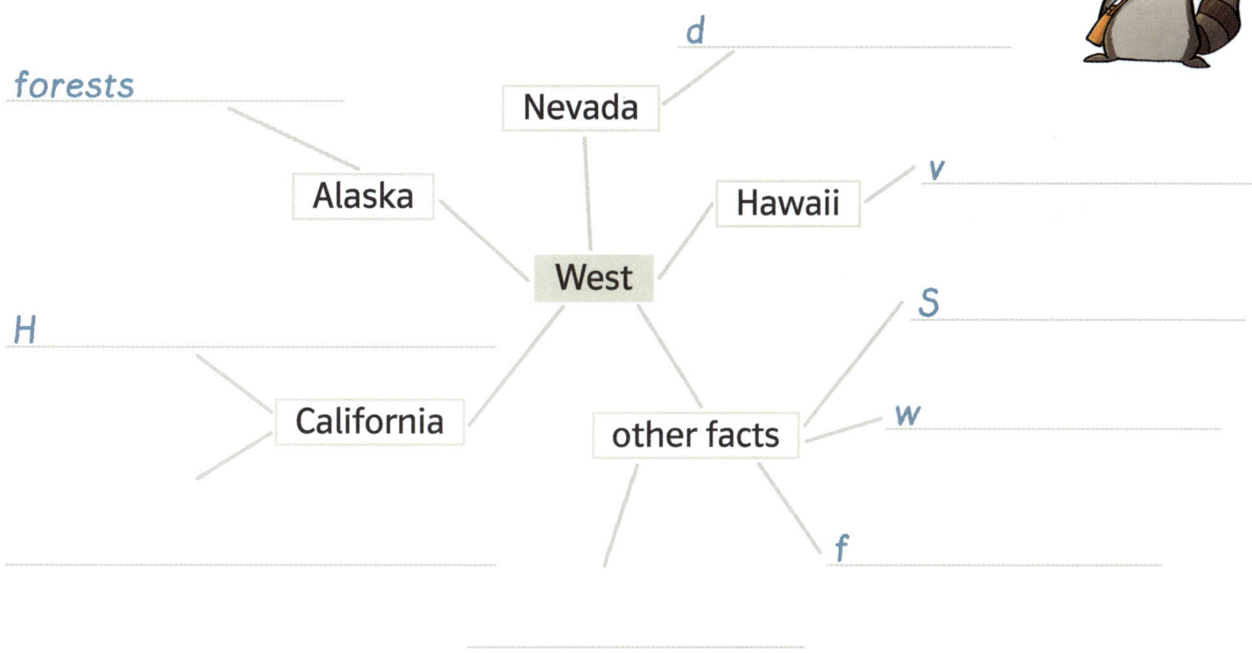

b) Watch the film. Circle the right answers and add them to the mind map in a). Schau dir den Film an. Kreise die richtigen Antworten ein und ergänze sie in der Mindmap in a).

V 6

1. The fog is beautiful on the **Golden Gate Bridge** | **hills**.
2. The best months for **festivals** | **surfing** are March and November.

c) Talk about the West.
Sprich über den Westen.

Es hilft dir beim Vorlesen, wenn du die Sätze zuerst aufschreibst.

The West is popular for surfing.

for its fantastic landscapes | as Silicon Valley is there | …

The region is important because it's the centre for technology.

they produce a lot of fruit | …

But there are also a lot of wildfires.

volcanoes | very hot places | …

✓ Ich kann Informationen über den Westen verstehen.

The life of a phone

1 How many phones have you had? Wie viele Handys hast du gehabt?

I've had ... phones.

2 Read Luciana's blog entry. Lies Lucianas Blogeintrag. ► Vokabeln S. 126 (V5)

Internet

Hey guys,
Two months ago, I wanted to buy a new phone.
Did you know the average American only uses a phone for about two and a half years? The problem is that you need a lot of energy and raw materials to produce a phone.
It can also be really bad for the environment if you throw it away.

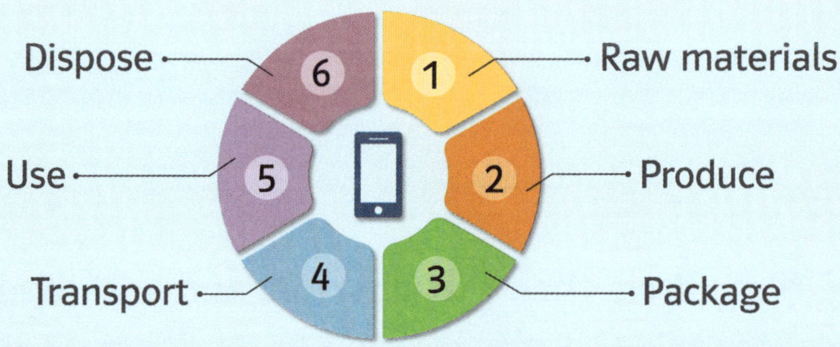

1 Phones are made of metals, plastics, and other materials. Metals are taken from under the ground.
2 Most phones are put together in large factories in China, and that needs a lot of energy.
3 Each phone is packaged with paper, card, and plastic.
4 Phones are transported around the world.
5 Most phones are used for three to four hours every day and charged for two to three hours.
6 More than 80 % of the world's phones are not recycled.

I think it's time for more sustainable phones. They are ...
✓ recycled. ✓ easy to repair.

What do you think? Leave a comment here.

3 Circle the right answers. Kreise die richtigen Antworten ein.

1. Two and a half years is the **average** | **shortest** time that people use their phones.
2. Metals for phones come from **under the ground** | **other factories**.
3. Most phones are made in **the USA** | **China**.
4. Companies use paper, card and plastic to **package** | **recycle** phones.
5. People use their phones **two to three hours every day** | **three to four hours every day**.
6. A sustainable phone **is better for the environment** | **doesn't need to be packaged**.

4 Match the pictures with the actions.
Ordne die Bilder den Tätigkeiten zu.

A

B

C

D

E

F

☐	program devices
☐	package things
A	produce devices
☐	transport products
☐	process metal
☐	mine raw materials

Language

Im Deutschen bildest du das Passiv mit **wird** oder **werden** und der dritten Verbform. Im Englischen ist das ähnlich: Du benutzt **is** oder **are** plus die dritte Verbform:

Die meisten Verben enden auf **ed**. Es gibt aber auch Ausnahmen, die du schon vom present perfect kennst.

You **package** each phone. → Each phone **is packaged**.
Du **verpackst** jedes Telefon. → Jedes Telefon **wird verpackt**.

They **don't recycle** many phones. → Many phones **aren't recycled**.
Sie **recyceln** viele Telefone **nicht**. → Viele Telefone **werden nicht recycelt**.

5 Complete the sentences.

Vervollständige die Sätze.

Ist die Handlung wichtiger als die Person, benutzt du das Passiv.

are processed | is programmed | are delivered | is ordered ✓ | are produced | are checked

1. The school robot *is ordered* .
2. The raw materials ______ .
3. The robots ______ .
4. Each robot ______ .
5. The robots ______ .
6. Then the robots ______ to the school.

6 Circle the right words. Kreise die richtigen Wörter ein.

1. Sustainable phones **are** | **aren't** made of new metals.
2. Important materials **are** | **aren't** thrown away.
3. A sustainable phone **is** | **isn't** exchanged after two years.
4. It **is** | **isn't** easily repaired.

7 Put the words in the right order to make questions.

Bringe die Wörter in die richtige Reihenfolge, um Fragen zu bilden.

1. is used to produce | a sustainable phone | How much energy | ?

   How much energy is ______________________________

2. are phones put | Where | together | ?

   ____

3. How | transported | is each phone | ?

   ____

8 Complete the sentences. Vervollständige die Sätze.

added | cooked | checked | collected ✓ | sold | prepared | cut | washed

A

First, the apples *are* __________ *collected* __________.

B

After that, they *are* __________ __________.

C

Then they *are* __________ __________ and they *are* __________.

D

The apples *are* __________ __________ and sugar *is* __________.

E

Then the apple jam *is* __________ for sale.

Hier ist ein unregelmäßiges Verb, das du schon vom present perfect kennst: cut → cut → **cut** (geschnitten).

9 **Your turn:** The life cycle of a product

Create a diagram to show the life cycle of a product.

Erstellt ein Diagramm, um den Lebenszyklus eines Produkts zu zeigen.

Step 1: Decide on a product.
Entscheidet euch für ein Produkt.

clothes, TVs, consoles, toys, ...

Step 2: Find out about the life cycle of the product. Take notes.
Recherchiert den Lebenszyklus des Produkts. Macht euch Notizen.
- raw materials (Rohstoffe)
- produce (produzieren)
- use (benutzen)
- dispose (entsorgen)

The life cycle of a shirt
- *raw materials: cotton (USA, India, China), water, dyes*
- *produce the fabrics (wash cotton, dye and process it) and the shirt (cut and sew it)*
- *use it for less than a year*
- *dispose of it or give it away*

Step 3: Draw a circle and four lines to divide it into four parts. Those are the stages of the life cycle.
Zeichnet einen Kreis und vier Linien, um ihn in vier Teile zu teilen. Das sind die Phasen des Lebenszyklus'.

Media tip
Erstellt eine neue Datei in einer Präsentationssoftware. Kreise und andere Formen findet ihr dort meist unter „Einfügen".

Step 4: Use text boxes to add your notes from step 2.
Erstellt Textkästen, um eure Notizen von Step 2 einzufügen.

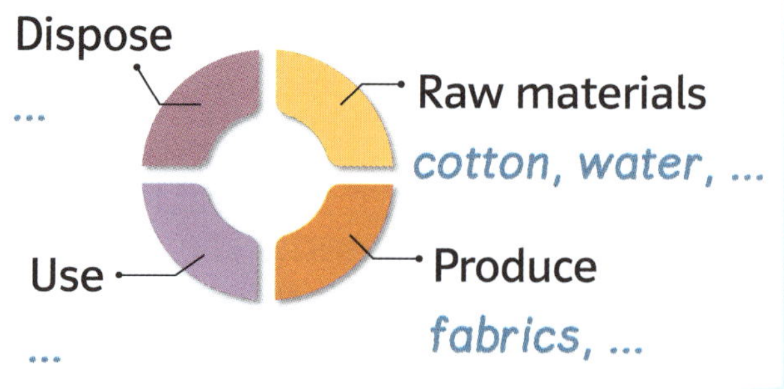

Step 5: Add symbols for each stage.
Fügt Symbole für jede Phase hinzu.

✓ Ich kann über den Lebenszyklus eines Produkts sprechen.

Climate heroes

1 Complete the sentences. Vervollständige die Sätze.

detect | global | engineer | connection | solution ✓

1. A *solution* ________ is the answer to a problem.
2. There's a ________ between a healthy forest and good air.
3. Football is a ________ sport.
4. Metal detectors can ________ weapons.
5. My uncle is an ________. He repairs and checks computers.

2 Watch the film. Match the right sentence parts.

V 7

Sieh dir den Film an. Verbinde die richtigen Satzteile.

1. The kids want to work on — because it has the same climate.
2. Their global connection is Spain — in Copenhagen.
3. The idea is to put up cameras — wildfires.
4. The kids show their project — in the forest that use solar energy.
5. Their solution is a screensaver — work with engineers.
6. The team who wins will — that shows you when there's a fire.

Culture
Die Waldbrandsaison in den USA geht von Frühling bis Herbst. Durch den Klimawandel gibt es aber auch im Winter immer öfter Waldbrände.

3 What should or shouldn't you do in a forest?

Was solltet ihr in einem Wald tun und was solltet ihr nicht tun?

take waste home | be quiet | light fires | feed animals | …

✓ Ich kann eine Reportage verstehen.

Your community needs you!

1 Read the conversation. Lies dir die Unterhaltung durch. ► Vokabeln S.127 (V6)

Lois is a student from Portland, Oregon. She's thinking about helping at Room to Hope, an outreach center for homeless people. She's talking to Bob, a member of staff at the center.

Lois So, what do you do at Room to Hope?

Bob We help homeless people in the city. Some members of staff know about medicine, others give advice and practical help.

Lois What's your job here?

Bob I'm here to find out about the homeless people's situation. I explain what they can do and help them to cope.

Lois What kind of help do you offer?

Bob Finding places to live is one of the most important things. I listen to them too. Most people just need a friend. And I ask about their health.

Lois That's really interesting. Why do people become homeless?

Bob There are different reasons. Often it's because they lose their jobs and can't pay their rent anymore. Sometimes it's because people get ill, take drugs or drink alcohol.

Lois What's the best thing about social work?

Bob Helping someone find a home and a job. Seeing them happy again is the best thing. It's my reason for doing this job.

Lois And what's the worst thing?

Bob Well, some people with strong drug or alcohol problems just can't stop forever. That's really difficult to see. And sometimes we can't help. That's very sad too.

Lois Okay. Thanks for talking to me.

2 Look up and write the meaning of the words.

Schlage die Bedeutung der Wörter nach und schreibe sie auf.

1. homeless *obdachlos*
2. practical ______
3. to cope ______
4. to offer ______
5. rent ______

Du kannst zum Nachschlagen entweder ein gedrucktes Wörterbuch, das Internet oder eine App benutzen.

3 What does Room to Hope do? Match the words.

Was tut Room to Hope?
Verbinde die Wörter.

1. It gives ———	advice and practical help.
2. It finds	what homeless people can do.
3. It explains	a place to live for them.
4. It helps	their health.
5. It asks about	homeless people to cope.

4 Listen to Arthur's story. Are the sentences true or false?

A 11

Höre dir Arthurs Geschichte an. Sind die Sätze wahr oder falsch?

	true	false
1. Arthur never had a job.	☐	☑
2. He had a problem with alcohol.	☐	☐
3. He lived in his car.	☐	☐
4. It was easy for Arthur to stop drinking.	☐	☐
5. Now he helps to raise money for Room to Hope.	☐	☐

5 Mediation

Sprachmittlung: Deine Freundin Nadja bringt dir diesen Flyer. Sie versteht aber nur wenig Deutsch. Vervollständige die englische Zusammenfassung für sie.

Du weißt nicht, wo du schlafen sollst?
Schule oder Ausbildung geschmissen?
Kein Geld, keinen Plan und niemand da, der dir hilft?

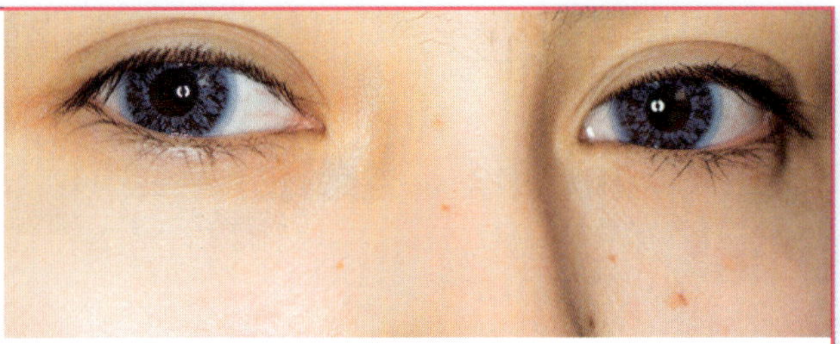

Keine Angst – es gibt Menschen, die sich damit auskennen!
Egal, ob online, am Telefon oder Face-to-Face: Wir helfen dir – ganz vertraulich und kostenlos.

Für wen gibt es Hilfe?
- Du bist zwischen 14 und 26.
- Du bist oder wirst wohnungslos.

Worum geht's?
Darum,
- dir zu helfen, ein selbstständiges Leben zu führen,
- eine passende Unterkunft zu finden, wenn du kein Zuhause mehr hast.

Wo bekommst du Hilfe?
- ✓ Wir kommen zu dir – auf die Straße, in Clubs, Chats oder wo auch immer du bist.
- ✓ Wir helfen dir bei der Wohnungssuche und begleiten dich, wenn du willst, auch zu anderen Hilfestellen.
- ✓ Brauchst du länger Hilfe, begleiten wir dich auch über mehrere Monate oder Jahre.

offer | free | no home ✓ | practical | a place to live | their own life

This service is for young people with *no home* ______ and no money. The goal is to help them live ______ and find them ______. Staff at the organisation ______ advice and ______ help online, on the phone, and face-to-face. The service is ______.

Language

Wenn du an ein Verb ein **ing** hängst, kannst du es wie ein Nomen benutzen. Im Deutschen würdest du ein „zu“ vor das Verb setzen:

Losing your home must be awful.
Dein Zuhause **zu verlieren**, muss furchtbar sein.

My friend is good at **speaking** to people.
Meine Freundin ist gut darin, mit Leuten **zu reden.**

6 Complete the description. Vervollständige die Beschreibung.

getting | making | learning | helping | working ✓

Hi, I'm Tessa. I'm a volunteer in a second-hand store.

I love *working* here.

I really enjoy ______ the customers.

I think I'm good at ______ them feel welcome.

I'm really interested in ______ a job in social work.

I'm looking forward to ______ more about social work.

7 Which of these activities would you do as a volunteer?

Welche dieser Aktivitäten würdet ihr ehrenamtlich tun?

playing with children | cooking | helping older people | cleaning | reading to people | …

A What are you good at doing?

B I'm good at listening to people.
What do you like doing?

A I like looking after animals and …

Culture

In den USA arbeiten viele Jugendliche ehrenamtlich. Das hilft ihnen später bei der Bewerbung um einen Studienplatz.

8 **Your turn:** A presentation about a social project

Give a three-minute group presentation about a social project that you want to raise money for. Haltet eine dreiminütige Präsentation zu einem sozialen Projekt, für das ihr Geld sammeln möchtet.

Step 1: Get into groups. Decide on a German social project.
Bildet Gruppen. Entscheidet euch für ein deutsches Sozialprojekt.

first aid club, animal home, outreach centre for …

Step 2: Research the project: Who does the project help? How does it help? How can you take part?
Recherchiert das Projekt: Wem hilft es? Wie hilft es? Wie kannst du mitmachen?

Breakfast club
- *help young people at school*
- *offer breakfast*
- *help make breakfast*
- *needs volunteers, money, food*
- *…*

Step 3: Show why this project is important.
Zeigt, warum das Projekt wichtig ist.

Everybody needs food, but some families don't have enough money for breakfast. That's where our project helps. …

Step 4: Write the rest of your presentation and add photos.
Schreibt den Rest eurer Präsentation und ergänzt Fotos.

Step 5: Decide who will say what. Practise your parts.
Entscheidet, wer was vorträgt. Übt eure Teile.

Our social project is the Breakfast club. It's a school project. We want to offer breakfast at school for students who don't have breakfast at home. You need volunteers who prepare the food at school and people who donate money or food. … What do you think?

Es gibt natürlich auch noch andere Möglichkeiten, wie ihr Projekten helfen könnt.

✓ Ich kann ein soziales Projekt vorstellen.

The gold rush

1 Match the words with the photos. Ordne die Wörter den Fotos zu.

ghost town | creek | luck | gold-mining tools

A

c

B

C

D

2 Life in Saint Elmo

A 12

a) Listen to the radio play. Put the photos in the right order.

Höre dir das Hörspiel an. Bringe die Fotos in die richtige Reihenfolge.

A

B

C

A 12

b) Listen again. Match the questions and answers.

Höre noch einmal zu. Verbinde die Fragen mit den Antworten.

1. Where do the tourists meet Owen?	There was no more work.
2. Why is Saint Elmo busier now?	In front of a store.
3. What did Carlos hope to find?	It was closed.
4. Why did people leave Saint Elmo?	Gold.
5. What happened to the school?	A lot of tourists are visiting.

✓ Ich kann ein Hörspiel verstehen.

A 13

America's natural treasures by Ava Jones, 04/20/2025

A The USA's 63 national parks are some of the country's most important areas. There are deserts, forests, canyons, and even volcanoes. In some parks you can find bison, wolves, and grizzly bears; other parks are home to many different kinds of birds and alligators.

B One of the first national parks in the USA was Yosemite in California. John Muir wanted to protect America's wilderness, but not everyone agreed. Muir wrote magazine articles about his ideas for Yosemite Valley. In 1890 the US Congress[1] decided to make a national park there.

C Today the National Park Service (NPS) takes care of all the national parks in the USA. The NPS makes the rules, looks after visitor facilities, and does research on how to protect the parks. It has about 20,000 employees[2] and 280,000 volunteers.

D Visitors must not leave any waste. They cannot take anything from the parks home with them except photos. Getting close to the animals or feeding them is not allowed either. Visitors should stay on the paths.

National parks: fascinating facts

The USA's largest national park is bigger than Switzerland. (Alaska)
The world's tallest tree is 380 feet high. (California)
In the early 1900s there were only 23 bison in Yellowstone National Park. Now there are around 5,000. (Montana, Wyoming & Idaho)
The coldest national park has temperatures as low as –70°F. (Alaska)

1 US Congress – *der US-Kongress*; 2 employee – *der/die Angestellte*

1 Read the text and find the information.

Lies den Text und finde die Informationen.

1. three different **landscapes**: *deserts,* ....
2. three **animals**: ....
3. **where** one of the first national parks in the US is: ....
4. one **fact** you find **interesting**: ....

2 Match the headings with the paragraphs of the text.

Ordne die Überschriften den Absätzen im Text zu.

1. Managing the national parks — That's *paragraph C.*
2. Different landscapes, animals and plants ....
3. Information for visitors ....
4. The past ....

3 What information is on the posters about national parks?

Welche Informationen enthalten die Poster über Nationalparks?

water | a forest | mountains | a canyon | ...

yellow | brown | blue | white | ...

cold | hot | big | exciting | boring | ...

On poster A there are a sun and ... .
The colours are ... .
The national park looks ... .

On poster B there is/are ... .
...

A

B

✓ Ich kann einen Zeitschriftenartikel verstehen.

Checklist

Complete eight facts about the West of the USA.

Vervollständige acht Fakten zum Westen der USA.

surfing | deserts ✓ | a lot of fruit | the world's tallest tree | gold rush | forests | technology | ghost town

A

Some of the fantastic landscapes in the West are the volcanoes in Hawaii, the *deserts* ________ in Nevada and the ________________ in Alaska.

B

The world's center for ________________ is Silicon Valley in California. California's coast is famous for ________________ too.

C

The West produces ________________ like apples and cherries. Many people work on fruit farms.

D

The year 1880 was the beginning of the ________ ________________. Saint Elmo was important for gold mining. Now it's a ________________.

E

The Redwood National Park in California is one of 63 national parks in the US. You can see ________ ________________ there. It's 380 feet high.

Task: A slide show

Prepare a slide show to present a German national park.

Bereitet eine Slideshow über einen deutschen Nationalpark vor.

Step 1: Read the rules. Lest die Regeln.

- 10 slides
- 1 picture per slide (1 Bild pro Folie); no text (kein Text)
- 20 seconds per slide (jede Folie wird für 20 Sekunden gezeigt)

Step 2: Get into groups. Choose a German national park. Find out ...

- **where** and **how big** it is (wo? wie groß?),
- **how old** it is (wie alt?),
- what **wildlife** and **plants** you can find there (Wildtiere? Pflanzen?),
- what visitors can **do** there (was tun?),
- what **challenges** there are (Herausforderungen?).

Hainich
- *Thuringia*
- *about 75 square kilometres*
- *built in 1997*
- *in the past the army used parts of it*
- *...*

Step 3: Make notes: What information do you want to give with which slide?
Notiert euch: Welche Informationen wollt ihr zu welcher Folie geben?

Slide 1: place and size
Thuringia, about 75 square kilometres

Step 4: Make your slide show. Decide who will present which part. Then practise.
Erstellt eure Slideshow. Entscheidet, wer welchen Teil vorstellt. Dann übt.

Media tip
Es gibt verschiedene Arten, etwas bildlich darzustellen, z. B. Fotos, Diagramme, Symbole, ...

Fang mit einem Slide an. Du kannst mit einer Stoppuhr testen, wie viel du in 20 Sekunden sagen kannst. Wenn du dich sicher fühlst, übe mehrere Slides hintereinander.

A look at Alaska

1 What do you already know about Alaska?

Was weißt du schon über Alaska?

1

1 Geography

Alaska is a state of forests, rivers, lakes, mountains, ice, and volcanoes.
But the ice is melting[1] because of the warming climate. There are also more wildfires in the forests.

1 to melt – *schmelzen*

2 Facts

Alaska is the largest state in the USA, but only about 733,000 people live there.
In the past Alaska was part of Russia. In 1867 Russia sold the region to the USA for $7.2 million.
Anchorage is the biggest city in Alaska, but Juneau is the state capital.

2

3 Nature

Alaska is a great place to see wildlife. Whale watching is very popular. Visitors to Denali National Park can see eagles[2], caribou[3], and grizzly bears.
The Northern Lights[4] are fantastic too.

2 eagle – *der Adler*
3 caribou – *das Rentier, die Rentiere*
4 the Northern Lights – *die Polarlichter*

4 Alaska Native people

There are many different Native American groups in Alaska. Traditionally they hunted and fished[5], and used dog sleds[6]. Sometimes dog sleds are still used today.

5 to fish – *fischen*
6 dog sled – *der Hundeschlitten*

2 Would you like to live in Alaska? Say why.

Würdet ihr gerne in Alaska leben? Sagt, warum.

there are a lot of wild animals | it's very cold | …

having dog sleds | seeing the Northern Lights | …

cool | beautiful | boring | lonely | …

A I would/wouldn't like to live in Alaska because there aren't many people there.

B I think … would/wouldn't be … .

Flags in the West

Complete the sentences and the crossword with the right places.

Vervollständige die Sätze und das Kreuzworträtsel mit den richtigen Orten.

Alaska | California ✓ | Colorado | Nevada | San Francisco

1. Silicon Valley is in *California* ____________.

1

2. The largest state in the USA is ____________.

2

3. The ghost town Saint Elmo is in ____________.

3

4. The Golden Gate Bridge is in ____________.

4

5. There are deserts in ____________.

5

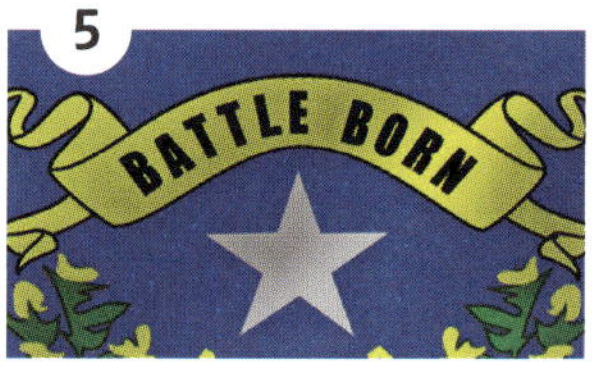

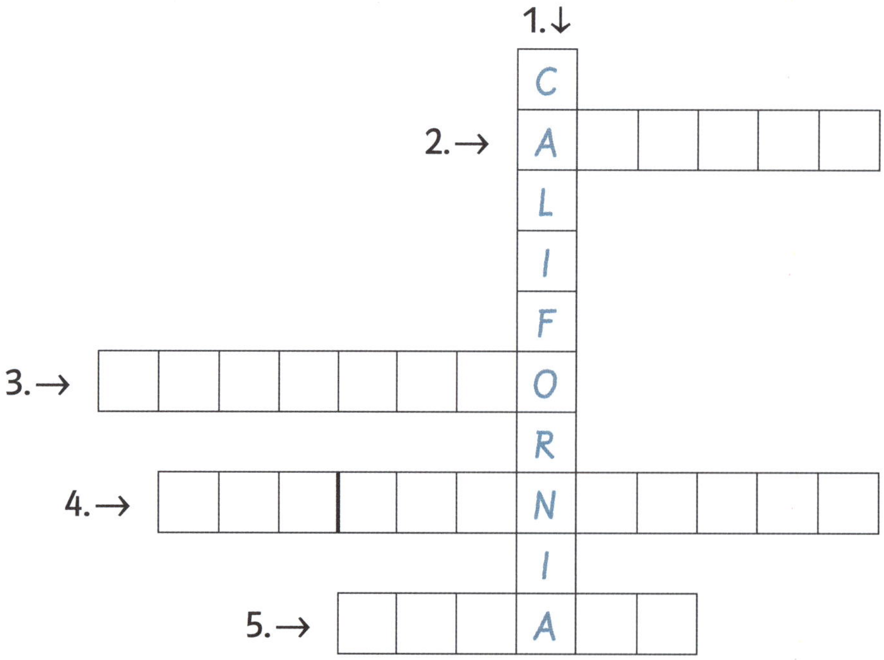

Social work

Die deutschen Wörter auf der rechten Seite brauchst du erst in Aufgabe 2.

1 Match the yellow words with the right green words and write them down.

Ordne den gelben Wörtern die richtigen grünen Wörter zu und schreibe sie auf. ► Vokabeln S.127 (V6)

outreach ✓ | drug | pay | homeless | drink | raise | social

money | problems | work | alcohol | centre ✓ | rent | people

1	*outreach centre*	Obdachlose
2.	....	Beratungsstelle
3.	....	Sozialarbeit
4.	....	Alkohol trinken
5.	....	Drogenprobleme
6.	....	Miete bezahlen
7.	....	Geld sammeln

2 Match the words in exercise 1 with their German meaning.

Verbinde die Begriffe in Übung 1 mit ihrer deutschen Bedeutung.

3 Complete Lois' diary entry with words from exercise 1.

Vervollständige Lois' Tagebucheintrag mit Wörtern aus Aufgabe 1.

Today I met Bob. He works at Room to Hope, an O _ _ _ _ _ _ _ C _ _ _ _ _. Bob listens to H _ _ _ _ _ _ _ P _ _ _ _ _ and helps them to find a job or a place to live. Some people are homeless because they are ill. A lot of them lost their jobs and can't P _ _ their R _ _ _ anymore. That's very sad. I'd like to R _ _ _ _ M _ _ _ _ with friends to help Bob's team. They do a great job there.

4 Around the Southwest

In dieser Unit wirst du ...
- etwas über den Südwesten erfahren.
- ein Vorbild beschreiben.
- ein Filmporträt anschauen.
- über lokale Themen sprechen.
- Vorträge über das Berufsleben anhören.
- eine Kurzgeschichte lesen.

A

B

There are many deserts and canyons like the Grand Canyon here. The days can be very hot and the nights cold.

INFO

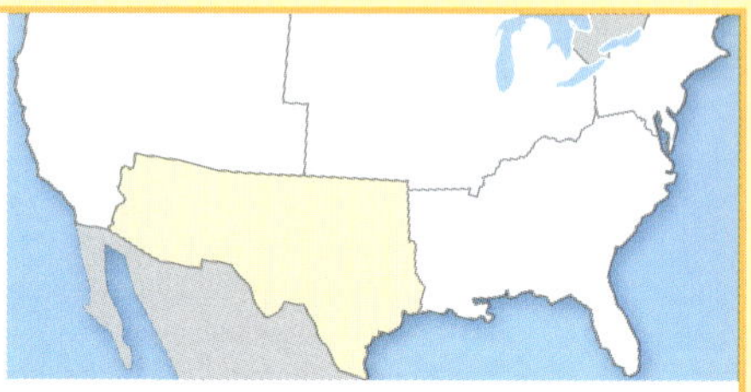

Biggest city: Houston, about 2.3 million people
Sights: Monument Valley, Acoma Pueblo, Old Town Albuquerque

C

The Navajo have their own schools and police. They're one of the USA's largest Native American groups.

D

Much of the Southwest was part of Mexico until 1848. That's why a lot of Hispanic people live there today.

E

The Hoover Dam is 726 feet high and 1,244 feet wide. It produces power for Nevada, Arizona, and California.

F

In the past cowboys used horses when they worked with cattle. Now cowboy skills are a sport at rodeos.

1 Facts about the Southwest

a) Read the texts. Add the words to the table.
Lies die Texte. Ergänze die Wörter in der Tabelle.

Du ergänzt zwei Stichpunkte erst in Aufgabe b).

hot days, cold nights | many Hispanic people | rodeos | power for three states | Navajo schools and police

climate	*mostly dry,*
landscapes	*deserts,*
people and culture	*the Navajo,*
economy	*the Hoover Dam:*
other facts	*cowboys worked with cattle,*

V 8

b) Watch the film. Tick the right answers and add them to the table in a). Schau dir den Film an. Setze ein Häkchen bei den richtigen Antworten und ergänze sie in der Tabelle in a).

1. Arizona has ☐ fire rivers ☐ trees that have turned to stone.
2. At the Grand Canyon you can see ☐ blue trees ☐ colourful rocks.

c) Talk about the Southwest.
Sprich über den Südwesten.

Es hilft dir beim Vorlesen, wenn du die Sätze zuerst aufschreibst.

The Southwest is interesting because of its extreme temperatures.

the Hoover Dam | cowboys | …

It's important to know that the Navajo have their own police and schools.

many states were part of Mexico | …

Visitors love the Grand Canyon.

rodeo shows | many cultures | …

✓ Ich kann Informationen über den Westen verstehen.

My role models

1 Read Julie's blog post. Lies Julies Blogeintrag. ► Vokabeln S.127 (V7)

Internet

Who inspires you?

by Julie

Have you ever thought about your role models? Here are mine:

My first role model is Emma Stone because she's very talented and strong. From a young age, she wanted to become an actor. But it wasn't easy. She didn't get many roles at first. Now she's a famous actor and has won many awards. She's inspired me to never give up.

My second role model is my high school sports coach, Mr. Morales. I never thought I was good at sports. But Mr. Morales saw that I could jump very high. He encouraged me to become a member of the high school team. Mr. Morales was very patient. He really helped us to become stronger. Because of him, I've become much more confident and ambitious.

Then there's my friend Becky from school. Becky is a little person. She's only four feet tall and has short arms and legs. At first people were awful to Becky, but she stood up to them. Life has sometimes been difficult for her, but she's always been positive. She's shown me that life is what you make it.

Who has inspired you?

Emma Stone

Mr. Morales

Becky

2 Match the statements with the role models.

Ordne die Aussagen den Vorbildern zu.

1. He/She isn't as tall as other people her age: *Becky*
2. He/She encouraged Julie: ______
3. He/She wasn't successful at first: ______
4. He/She is Julie's friend: ______

3 Find the descriptions in the text. Finde die Beschreibungen im Text.

1. two words to describe Emma Stone: *talented, strong*
2. one word to describe Mr Morales: ______
3. two words to describe Julie: ______
4. one word to describe Becky: ______

4 Match the definitions with the right adjectives.

Ordne den Definitionen die richtigen Adjektive zu.

1. not giving up	ambitious
2. practising a lot	patient
3. waiting for something	strong
4. believing in yourself	confident

5 Talk about three important qualities that a role model should have.

Sprecht über drei wichtige Eigenschaften, die ein Vorbild haben sollte.

talented | nice | positive | encouraging | smart | …

A I think role models should be ambitious, successful and … .

B I agree / I don't agree. I think being … is more important.

C I don't think a role model must be … .

The movie has started, but Mia hasn't arrived yet.

Language

Wenn etwas in der Vergangenheit angefangen hat und die Gegenwart beeinflusst, benutzt du **have** oder **has** und die dritte Verbform:

Becky **has inspired** me.	Becky **hat** mich **inspiriert**.
We **haven't won** anything yet.	Wir **haben** noch **nichts gewonnen**.
Have you ever **talked** to her?	**Hast** du jemals mit ihr **geredet**?

6 Match the sentence parts. Verbinde die Satzteile.

1. Emma Stone
2. She has already
3. She hasn't
4. Julie and Becky

- directed a film yet.
- haven't watched Emma's new film yet.
- has played different characters.
- worked with other famous actors.

7 Say what you have (✓) and haven't (✗) done today.

Sage, was du heute getan (✓) und was du nicht getan hast (✗).

A

I *haven't* ________ taken the dog for a walk yet.

B

I ________ read any books yet.

C

I ________ already eaten lunch.

D

I ________ played the guitar yet.

E

I ________ been at school all day.

F

I ________ talked to Julie too.

8 Complete the interview. Vervollständige das Interview.

have | Have you ever lost | has always seen | haven't
who has inspired | Have you always been ✓

Julie Hi Coach. Can I ask you some questions for my blog?

Coach Sure!

Julie *Have you always been* .... a track and field coach?

Coach No, I .... I worked in a small company before.

Julie .... an important competition?

Coach Yes, I .... It was a year ago.

Julie And .... you the most?

Coach My dad. He .... the best in me.

9 Underline the forms of the present perfect.

Unterstreiche die Perfekt-Formen.

Julie Look, it's the basketball player Dirk Nowitzki!

Becky Who? I've never heard of him.

Julie He was one of the greatest players ever.

Becky Where's he from?

Julie He was born in Germany, but he has lived in Dallas since 1998.

Becky What has he achieved?

Julie He has played in lots of important games. In 2007 he won the NBA Most Valuable Player Award.

Becky Wow! Has anyone written a book about him?

Julie Yes, a few people have written about him. I haven't read any of the books yet, but I'm going to soon.

10 **Your turn:** An email to a magazine

Write an email to the reporter Zara about your role model.

Schreibe der Reporterin Zara eine E-Mail über dein Vorbild.

Step 1: Choose a role model.
It can be someone famous or someone you know.
Suche dir ein Vorbild aus. Das kann jemand Berühmtes sein oder jemand, den oder die du kennst.

Media tip
Nicht jede Person, die viele Follower hat, ist ein geeignetes Vorbild. Manche verbreiten auch Hass, Vorurteile oder Lügen.

Step 2: Start with a greeting.
Introduce yourself and your role model.
Beginne mit einer Begrüßung.
Stelle dich und dein Vorbild vor.

Dear Zara,
My name is ... and I go to ... School. I read your article about role models and I would like to write about ... .

Step 3: Describe your role model.
What makes them special? How is their character? Give examples.
Beschreibe dein Vorbild. Was macht sie/ihn besonders? Was hat sie/er für einen Charakter? Gib Beispiele.

... has won / been / had ...
... is always very ambitious / confident / talented / ... .
... was very successful when ...
...

Step 4: Explain how your role model has influenced and inspired you.
Erkläre, wie dein Vorbild dich beeinflusst und inspiriert hat.

He / She has inspired me to be myself / follow my dreams / work harder / ... .
Because of him / her, I've become much more ... .

Step 5: Finish your email.
Schließe deine E-Mail ab.

... has been a big influence on me.
I think ... is a great role model.
Thank you and best wishes,
(Your full name)

✓ Ich kann ein Vorbild beschreiben.

Multicultural USA

1 Match the definitions with the words.

Verbinde die Definitionen mit den Wörtern.

1. where some Native Americans live, often not where they lived in the past
2. what you are allowed to do
3. someone who isn't free and has to work for other people
4. treating people badly because of their skin colour

reservation

slave

racism

rights

2 Watch the film. Complete the sentences.

V 9

Sieh dir den Film an. Vervollständige die Sätze.

slaves | reservations | Settlers ✓ | racism | rights

1. *Settlers* and diseases killed many Native Americans.
2. Now most of them live in towns, cities and on ______.
3. People from Africa were taken to America as ______.
4. Slaves were officially freed in 1865, but they didn't have the same ______ as other Americans.
5. There is still ______ today.

Culture

Der Februar ist in den USA der „Black History Month". In diesem Monat finden Veranstaltungen statt, die die Geschichte und Kultur dunkelhäutiger Menschen feiern und ihren Beitrag zum amerikanischen Leben würdigen. Es gibt auch z. B. den „Native American Heritage Month" und den „Hispanic Heritage Month" (heritage – das Erbe).

✓ Ich kann eine Reportage verstehen.

Life in a small town

1 Read what people say at a town hall meeting. Lies dir durch, was Leute bei einer Bürgerversammlung sagen. ► Vokabeln S. 128 (V8)

Host Thank you for coming. Our mayor is here to listen to you and answer your questions. First is high school student Pablo Ramirez.

Pablo Hello. Other cities have special graffiti walls where people can be creative. Our art class would like to have a wall like that too. Can Mayor Sanchez support this?

Mayor Good evening Mr. Ramirez. I can't say yes right now, but we can think about this when we make our plan for next year.

Host Our next speaker is Jason Allister, an engineer.

Jason My friends and I would like to improve our town's air quality. We'd like to plant 1,000 new trees. We want to plant them along sidewalks and around public places like the library and the hospital. The air will be better and the summers will be cooler. What does the mayor think?

Mayor This is a wonderful idea. I'm happy to say that we've already planned to plant around 500 new trees over the next five years.

2 Complete the report. Vervollständige den Bericht.

town hall ✓ | plans | graffiti wall | air quality

Internet

Last night's town hall meeting

At the *town hall* ______ meeting last night, a high school student asked for a ______.
An engineer and his friends want to achieve better ______ by planting trees.
The mayor said they already have ______ for that.

Mayor Elena Sanchez

3 Match the words with the pictures. Ordne die Wörter den Bildern zu.

bank | graffiti wall ✓ | hospital | sidewalk | hairdresser's | mayor

A

B

C

graffiti wall ______ ______

D

E

F
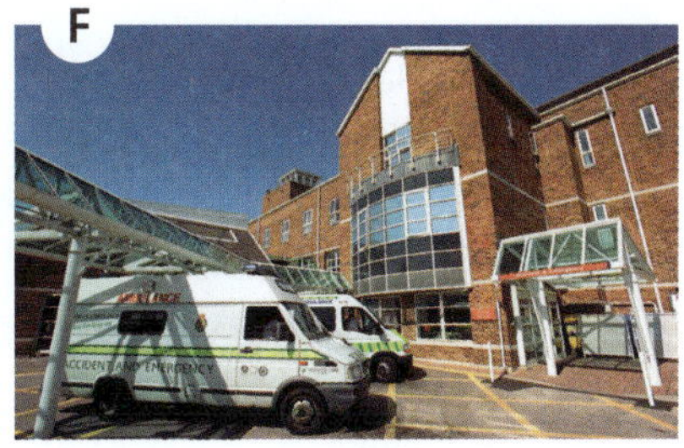

______ ______ ______

4 Add the words to the mind map. Ergänze die Wörter in der Mindmap.

basketball court | hairdresser's | bank | graffiti wall | train station | cinema | library | pool | hospital

In a town or city
- transport
  - *bus stop*
  - ______
- shops and services
  - ______
  - ______
- entertainment
  - ______
  - ______
- public buildings
  - ______
  - ______
  - *police station*
- sports facilities
  - *gym*
  - ______
  - ______

A 14

5 Listen to the interview. Tick the right answers.

Höre dir das Interview an. Setze Häkchen bei den richtigen Antworten.

1. Who were the first people who lived in Show Low?

☐ Spanish people ☐ Native Americans

2. What did Corydon Cooley and Marion Clark start together?

☐ a store ☐ a farm

3. When did they play a game?

☐ three years later ☐ five years later

4. Who won the game?

☐ Corydon Cooley ☐ Marion Clark

5. Who opened the first store in the area?

☐ Corydon Cooley ☐ Marion Clark

6 Look at the cartoon and answer the questions.

Schau dir den Cartoon an und beantworte die Fragen.

1. Who or what is in the cartoon?

There are a lot of *skyscrapers and cars.*

There's ______________________

The text is saying "______________________

______________________"

2. What does the cartoon tell you about big cities?

There are a lot of skyscrapers and cars, but

____

"You can't miss me – I'm under the tree."

Language

Die Wörter **since** und **for** bedeuten beide „seit", aber du benutzt **since** wenn etwas seit einem Zeitpunkt ● geschieht und **for** wenn es um einen Zeitraum ↔ geht:

The air quality has been bad **since 2010**.
Die Luftqualität ist **seit 2010** schlecht.

The air quality has been bad **for many years**.
Die Luftqualität ist **seit vielen Jahren** schlecht.

Du kannst den i-Punkt von since als Merkhilfe nehmen: **since** mit **i-Punkt** verwendest du für einen Zeit**punkt**.

7 Match the sentences with the right category.

Ordne die Sätze der richtigen Kategorie zu.

Zeitpunkt ●	Zeitraum ↔
1	

1. Jason and his friends have helped to plant 100 trees **since** April.
2. Elena has been the mayor of the town **since** 2018.
3. Maria has closed her shop **for** two days.
4. Pablo has won two art awards **since** last year.
5. The air quality has been OK **for** three weeks now.

8 Put the words in the right order.

Bringe die Wörter in die richtige Reihenfolge.

1. Pablo | since | has painted | September. | a lot of pictures

   Pablo has painted

2. his aquarium | two years. | He | for | has had

3. since | at school | Monday. | He | hasn't been

9 **Your turn:** Statements about local topics

Make statements about topics that are important in your city, town or village. Sagt etwas zu Themen, die in eurer Stadt oder in eurem Dorf wichtig sind.

Step 1: Work in groups.
What would you like to change or improve?
Arbeitet in Gruppen. Was möchtet ihr ändern oder verbessern?

transport
sports facilities
place(s) for people who like …
…

Step 2: Agree on a topic.
Collect arguments and examples.
Einigt euch auf ein Thema.
Sammelt Argumente und Beispiele.

Transport
- *not enough buses at weekend*
- *buses too full at other times*
- *…*

Step 3: Prepare a statement.
Bereitet eine Stellungnahme vor.
1. introduction (Einleitung)
2. arguments and statements (Argumente und Aussagen)
3. suggestion (Vorschlag)

The speaker will have one minute to talk.

Have you ever missed your bus and waited an hour for the next one? We have.
Our town doesn't have enough buses. Let me explain this.
First, …
The buses are also too …
Finally, …
This is why we believe that our town should have more buses.

Step 4: Decide who will be the speaker. Practise in your group.
Entscheidet euch, wer vorträgt.
Übt in eurer Gruppe.

✓ Ich kann über lokale Themen sprechen.

Finding out about jobs

1 Read the questions. Talk about your answers with a partner.

Lest die Fragen. Besprecht eure Antworten zu zweit.

1. What kind of job are you interested in?
   - working with people
   - working in an office
   - making things
   - working outside

2. What would you like to do?
   - work in a team
   - help people
   - study for a degree
   - do an apprenticeship
   - get a lot of money
   - use computers

A I'm interested in … .

B I'd like to … .

2 Listen to three people. Tick their jobs.

A 15

Höre drei Personen zu. Setze Häkchen bei ihren Jobs.

A
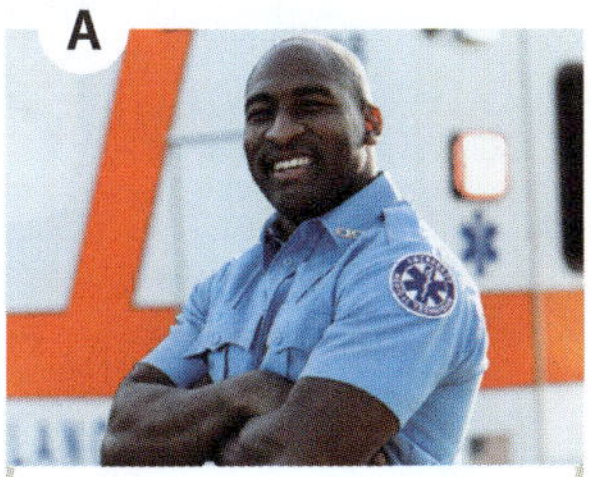
EMT ☐

B

electrician ☐

C

software engineer ☐

D
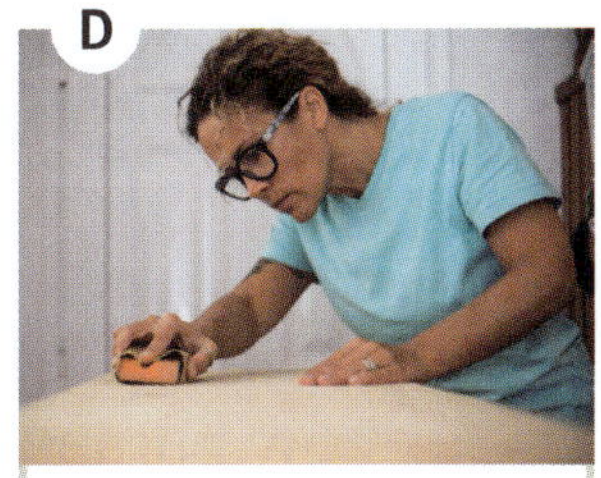
carpenter ☐

3 Listen again. Are the sentences true or false?

A 15

Höre noch einmal zu. Sind die Sätze wahr oder falsch?

	true	false
1. Gina did an apprenticeship for three years.	☐	☐
2. Ricardo sometimes has to work at night.	☐	☐
3. Ricardo's job never makes him sad.	☐	☐
4. Jenna studied for a degree.	☐	☐
5. Jenna often finishes work early.	☐	☐

✓ Ich kann Vorträge über das Berufsleben verstehen.

A 16

When everything changed

Beep beep, beep beep, went the alarm on Robert's phone.
Robert reached out for it. But something felt different.
When he pulled the covers[1] up, he was shocked. Robert was a girl!
He got up in a panic. His wardrobe was full of girls' clothes!
But he had to get dressed. He left the house and walked to the bus stop.
"Hey Nina! Nina!" shouted Ida and Hannah, two girls from Robert's class, when he got on the bus.
"Is that sweater new?" asked Ida. "I haven't seen it before."
"I don't know," answered Robert.
"And no make-up[2] today," added Hannah. "Cool natural look[3]!"
Robert felt confused and nervous.
Suddenly he understood. He was a girl called Nina, and to his friends, he'd always been Nina. It was crazy!

The school day started as always.
Sara invited Robert to sit next to her. He'd always liked her. Robert enjoyed how Sara was more friendly now than when he was a boy.
After lunch his friend Freddie stopped him.
"Hey Nina. Can I talk to you?" asked Freddie.
"I really like this girl, but I don't know how to tell her."
"Really?" asked Robert.
"Yeah, I've wanted to ask her on a date for weeks, but I feel really shy."
Robert was surprised. He thought Freddie was really confident and had kissed lots of girls. Robert saw that everyone treated him differently as a girl, and it wasn't too bad.
"I think it's best to be honest about how you feel," he told Freddie.
"Just be yourself. I'm sure she'll say yes," he added, smiling at his friend.
Freddie smiled back. Suddenly, Freddie moved his head forward and …

1 covers – *das Bettzeug*; 2 make-up – *das Make-up*; 3 look – *das Aussehen*

1 Read the short story and complete the sentences.
Lies die Kurzgeschichte und vervollständige die Sätze.

1. When Robert wakes up, he's a *girl* ______.
2. When he reaches for his phone, he feels *d* ______.
3. He learns that his name is *N* ______.
4. Robert *l* ______ Sara.
5. After lunch Freddie wants to *t* ______ to Robert.

2 Answer these questions with your own ideas.
Beantwortet diese Fragen mit euren eigenen Ideen.

Überlegt euch, welche Antworten passen könnten. Eure Ideen sollten zu den Ereignissen oder Personen in der Geschichte passen.

1. Why is Robert's house empty?
   A I think maybe Robert's house is empty because his parents are on holiday / are at work / … .
   B That's a good idea. / I don't think so. I think his parents are gone because it's a scary story / … .
2. What does Robert think when he looks at his clothes?
   A Maybe he thinks 'What are these colours?' / …
   B That's possible. / I don't think so. He probably thinks 'Where do all these girls clothes come from?' / … .
3. What do Freddie and Robert usually talk about?
   A I'm sure they talk about computer games / football / … .
   B That's right! / I don't agree. I think they talk about comics / films / … .

✓ Ich kann eine Kurzgeschichte verstehen.

Checklist

What have or haven't they done yet? Complete the sentences.

Was haben sie schon oder noch nicht gemacht? Vervollständige die Sätze.

has already visited | has hurt | hasn't been | has already finished | have already won ✓ | hasn't done | have already built | hasn't seen

A

Kira and Malea are very good at sports. They play basketball in the local team. They *have already won* some important awards.

B

Malea also loves travelling. She ______ the West and the Southwest of the US, but she ______ New York yet.

C

Kira's parents work as carpenters. They love their job, and they ______ some fantastic tables and chairs.

D

Today, Kira is at home because she isn't feeling well. She ______ to school since Monday. She ______ her foot badly.

E

Malea wants to visit Kira soon. She ______ her English exercises, but she ______ her Maths homework yet.

Task: A podcast

Record a short podcast about the Southwest.

Nehmt einen kurzen Podcast über den Südwesten auf.

Step 1: Get into groups and decide on your topic.

Bildet Gruppen und entscheidet euch für ein Thema.

Step 2: Research your topic. You should include three interesting aspects. Find two or three facts for each aspect.

Recherchiert euer Thema. Ihr solltet drei interessante Punkte erwähnen. Findet für jeden Punkt zwei bis drei Fakten.

Step 3: Write the script for your podcast.

Schreibt das Skript für euren Podcast.

Step 4: Practise your podcast. Decide who will speak when and who will check the recording.

Übt euren Podcast.
Entscheidet, wer wann spricht und wer die Aufnahme überprüft.

Step 5: Record your podcast.

Nehmt euren Podcast auf.

Hier sind ein paar Ideen: Tier- und Pflanzenwelt, Geschichte, berühmte Menschen, Sport, Wahrzeichen.

Natural sights in the Southwest:

1. The Grand Canyon
- *What and where is it?*
- *How long is it?*
- *...*

Welcome to our podcast about ... . I'm ... and this is ... .
Did you know that ...?
That's bigger than ... / twice as big as ...! Isn't that amazing?
...
Thanks for listening to our podcast. Goodbye!

Media tip

Du kannst dir in einem Online-Wörterbuch anhören, wie Wörter ausgesprochen werden.

The Southwest – deserts and more

1 Do you know the places and things in the photos?

Kennst du die Orte und Dinge in den Fotos?

1

1 Monument Valley is in the desert on the Arizona-Utah border[1]. It is famous for its tall rocks. The valley[2] is a sacred[3] place for the Navajo Nation who live in the area. It has also been in many movies.

1 border – *die Grenze*
2 valley – *das Tal*
3 sacred – *heilig*

2 Taos Pueblo is an old Native American village in New Mexico. About 150 people live there today. Most of the buildings are between 600 and 1,000 years old. The buildings have influenced the architecture[4] in Santa Fe and other cities.

4 architecture – *die Architektur*

2

3 The **Gila Monsters** live in the deserts and forests of the Southwest. They are venomous[5] and can bite[6]. Fortunately[7], they are slow and heavy, and they don't often attack[8] people.

5 venomous – *giftig*
6 to bite – *beißen*
7 fortunately – *zum Glück*
8 to attack – *angreifen*

4 Southwestern food is popular in many parts of the USA. Many dishes have corn, beans[9], and lots of chili in them. Burritos, enchiladas, and nachos are also very popular.

9 bean – *die Bohne*

2 What was new in the texts? What did you find interesting?

Was war neu in den Texten? Was fandest du interessant?

Monument Valley is sacred | there are forests in the Southwest | there's an animal with "monster" in its name | …

I knew that burritos, enchiladas and nachos are popular everywhere.

I didn't know that movies were made in Monument Valley.

It's interesting that people still live in Taos Pueblo.

The Wild Southwest

1 Pictures

a) Write the words under the photos. Schreibe die Wörter unter die Fotos.

Pueblo | desert ✓ | Houston | cowboys | Navajo | Grand

A

D E S E R T

B

☐☐☐☐☐☐☐

C

☐☐☐☐☐
Canyon

D

Taos
☐☐☐☐☐☐

E

the
☐☐☐☐☐☐

F

☐☐☐☐☐☐☐

b) Complete the sentence with the letters from the grey boxes. Vervollständige den Satz mit den Buchstaben aus den grauen Kästchen.

Today, cowboys in the Southwest show their skills at R☐☐☐☐☐.

2 Match the sentences parts. Verbinde die Satzteile.

1. Great sights are the Grand Canyon and
2. In the canyons, it can be hot during the day
3. The region of the Southwest is home to
4. Millions of Hispanic people live

the Navajo Nation.
the Monument Valley.
in the Southwest too.
and very cold at night.

Unit quiz

1 Tick the right boxes. Setze Häkchen in die richtigen Kästchen.

1. The biggest city in the Southwest is …
   - **o** ☐ Santa Fe.
   - **e** ☑ Houston.
2. The climate is …
   - **l** ☐ cold and wet.
   - **s** ☐ dry and hot.
3. Much of the area was part of …
   - **s** ☐ a French colony.
   - **e** ☐ Mexico.
4. The Navajo Nation is …
   - **t** ☐ a large area in the Southwest.
   - **r** ☐ a Native American tribe.
5. They have their own …
   - **i** ☐ hospitals and cowboys.
   - **v** ☐ schools and police.
6. Visitors of the Southwest love …
   - **z** ☐ the graffiti walls.
   - **a** ☐ the Grand Canyon.
7. The Grand Canyon is famous for its …
   - **t** ☐ colourful rocks.
   - **g** ☐ beautiful rivers.
8. Monument Valley is home to …
   - **i** ☐ the Navajo Nation.
   - **d** ☐ a lot of cowboys.
9. The Hoover Dam produces …
   - **o** ☐ power for three states.
   - **a** ☐ fish for five states.
10. Burritos, enchiladas, nachos …
    - **s** ☐ are food for poor people.
    - **n** ☐ are popular in the Southwest.

2 Complete the sentence with the letters in front of the right facts.

Vervollständige den Satz mit den Buchstaben vor den richtigen Fakten.

Today, Native Americans live in towns, cities or on

r	e									s
	1	2	3	4	5	6	7	8	9	10

.

5 Settling in the South

In dieser Unit wirst du …
- etwas über den Süden erfahren.
- über Diskriminierung sprechen.
- einen Naturfilm anschauen.
- deine Meinung äußern.
- ein Radio-Feature anhören.
- einen Artikel aus einem Geschichtsmagazin lesen.

A

B

In Florida you can see the Everglades, an area with forests and lakes, and a launch site for space missions.

INFO

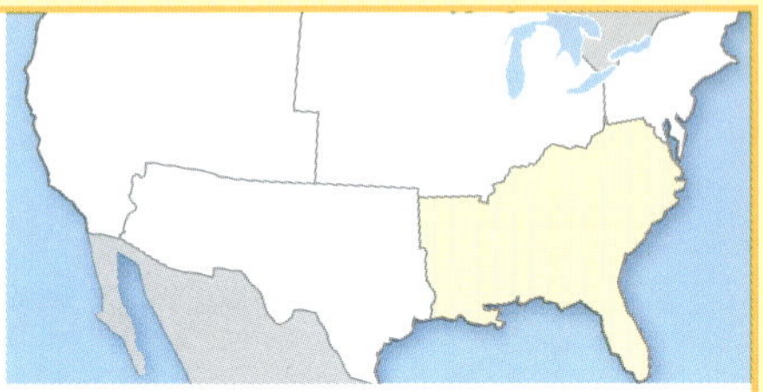

Biggest city: Jacksonville, about 970,000 people
Sights: Country Music Hall of Fame, Kennedy Space Center

C

The South is famous for its barbecue competitions. Many people are proud of this tradition.

D

French settlers founded New Orleans. For a while, it was Spanish. The city is famous for its Mardi Gras carnival.

E

The civil rights movement started in the 1950s. Black people protested against racism, which is still a problem.

F

The South coast is often hit by hurricanes. The storms start over the ocean and often damage buildings.

1 Read the texts. Add the words to the notes.

a) Lies die Texte. Ergänze die Wörter auf den Notizzetteln.

Everglades ✓ | space missions | racism | civil rights movement | Mardi Gras | barbecue competitions | French and Spanish settlers

Climate & landscapes
- *Everglades*
- ______
- ______

Traditions
- *M*______
- *b*______
  ______

Other facts
- *s*______
  ______
- *r*______

History
- *c*______
- *F*______

Zwei Linien beschreibst du erst in Aufgabe 1 b).

b) Watch the film. Circle the right words and add them to the notes in a). Schau dir den Film an. Kreise die richtigen Wörter ein und ergänze sie in den Notizen in a).

V 10

1. The Florida landscape has many **deserts** | **wetlands**.
2. Buildings can be damaged by **hurricanes** | **alligators**.

Es hilft dir beim Vorlesen, wenn du die Sätze zuerst aufschreibst.

c) Talk about the South. Sprich über den Süden.

The South is a region with many traditions. — big cities | hurricanes | a warm climate | …

In the past Black people started the civil rights movement there. — the French founded New Orleans | …

Today racism is still a problem. — there are barbecue competitions | …

✓ Ich kann Informationen über den Süden verstehen.

Respecting each other

1 Read the comments. Lies die Kommentare. ► Vokabeln S. 129 (V9)

Internet

Macy
Charlotte, North Carolina

When you treat someone unfairly because of what they look like or who they are … that's discrimination. This happens very often. I have a disability: I must use a wheelchair. Last week the elevator at my station didn't work, and I wasn't able to get to the platform. Most people just walked past me, although I asked for help. Some even pushed me out of their way and insulted me. Finally, three people helped me. What are your experiences of difficult situations? What did you do?

Jamar
Biloxi, Mississippi

I'm so sorry to hear that, Macy. I'm a person of color. Last month I worked at a summer camp. Most people were nice, but there were a boy and a girl who insulted me when we were alone. I felt helpless. But I ignored them, and they soon lost interest in me.

Ricarda
Savannah, Georgia

I really understand you. When I started school here in the USA, some of the other students thought I was stupid because I wasn't able to speak English very well. But I'm very good at volleyball. After some time in the team things got better. You mustn't give up!

Jin
Knoxville, Tennessee

When my mom first arrived here 20 years ago, she couldn't find a job. Her English was very good, but because she was Chinese and a woman, people didn't take her seriously. Together with other women she raises awareness of women's rights now.

2 What do these phrases mean in English? Underline them in the text.

Was bedeuten diese Sätze auf Englisch? Unterstreiche sie im Text.

Manche haben mich sogar aus dem Weg geschubst und mich beleidigt.

Ich habe mich hilflos gefühlt.

… ich konnte nicht besonders gut Englisch sprechen.

… sie macht jetzt auf Rechte von Frauen aufmerksam.

A 17

3 Listen and put the strategies in the right order.

Höre zu und bringe die Strategien in die richtige Reihenfolge.

A Don't make yourself small. ☐

B Remember that words can hurt. ☐

C Stay calm. 1

D Your health always comes first. ☐

A 18

4 Listen and say the words. Underline the parts with the stress.

Höre zu und sprich die Wörter nach. Unterstreiche die Betonungen.

1. educate – education
2. celebrate – celebration
3. discriminate – discrimination
4. present – presentation
5. invite – invitation
6. compete – competition
7. describe – description

Language

Wenn du sagen willst, dass du etwas tun **kannst**, **darfst** oder **musst**, verwendest du Verben wie **can**, **may** oder **must**.

They can use lifts.	Sie **können** Aufzüge benutzen.
They may use lifts.	Sie **dürfen** Aufzüge benutzen.
They must use lifts.	Sie **müssen** Aufzüge benutzen.

5 Complete the sentences.

Vervollständige die Sätze.

must study | may ride ✓ | can run | mustn't use | can't play | needn't wear

Achtung!
must → müssen
mustn't → nicht dürfen
needn't → nicht müssen

A

People *may ride* bikes here.

B

He ______________ ______________ the guitar very well yet.

C

You ______________ phones here.

D

Students ______________ ______________ a uniform.

E

He ______________ ______________ very fast.

F

They ______________ ______________ for their exams.

Language

In der Vergangenheit werden diese Verben zu ganz anderen Wörtern:

I **can** walk to school. → I **was able to** walk to school.
I **may** walk to school. → I **was allowed to** walk to school.
I **must** walk to school. → I **had to** walk to school.
I **mustn't** walk to school. → I **wasn't allowed to** walk to school.
I **needn't** walk to school. → I **didn't have to** walk to school.

6 Match the sentence parts. Verbinde die Satzteile.

1. As a child, Macy wasn't allowed to use	play in the park together.
2. But she and her friend were allowed to	the train alone.
3. Ricarda wasn't able to play	volleyball for three months.
4. Jamar had to look after	move to a new city.
5. Jin was happy that she didn't have to	his little brother last month.

7 Circle the right words.

Kreise die richtigen Wörter ein.

June 24

I'll go to college soon. I'll live in my own apartment. **I'll have to** | **I'll be able to** (must) cook and clean. **I'll have to** | **I'll be able to** (can) eat what I want. **I'll have to** | **I'll be able to** (must) get a job to pay for my car and my rent. **I'll have to** | **I'll be able to** (may) buy my own things and travel around. I'm really excited about the future!

Für die Zukunft verwendest du die gleichen Ersatzwörter, wie für die Vergangenheit – aber natürlich mit **will**:
I'**ll be able to**
I **won't be allowed to**
I'**ll have to**

8 **Your turn:** An anti-discrimination poster

Make a poster to show what to do against discrimination.

Erstellt ein Poster um zu zeigen, was man gegen Diskriminierung tun kann.

Step 1: How are people discriminated against? Collect examples.
Wie werden Menschen diskriminiert? Sammelt Beispiele.

Ihr müsst nicht über eigene Erfahrungen sprechen. Ihr könnt auch über die Erfahrungen von anderen sprechen.

Step 2: What can you do to fight discrimination? Collect ideas.
Was könnt ihr tun, um Diskriminierung zu bekämpfen? Sammelt Ideen.

- *talk to ...*
- *organise ...*

...

Step 3: Discuss what you want to achieve. Make notes.
Besprecht, was ihr erreichen wollt. Macht euch Notizen.

Was soll euer Poster bewirken? Anderen zeigen, was Diskriminierung ist? Gleiche Rechte für alle fordern? Werbung für eine Aktion machen?

Step 4: Search the internet for pictures.
Sucht im Internet nach Bildern.

Step 5: Make a first draft of the text. Arrange your pictures.
Schreibt einen ersten Entwurf eures Textes. Ordnet die Bilder an.

- *Respect other people!*
- *Stop discrimination!*
- ...

Step 6: Write the final text and add the pictures to your poster.
Schreibt den fertigen Text und ergänzt die Bilder auf eurem Poster.

✓ Ich kann über Diskriminierung sprechen.

A trip to the Everglades

1 Look up the words and write their German meaning.

Schlage die Wörter nach und schreibe ihre deutsche Bedeutung auf.

license *Lizenz; Erlaubnis*

sleeve

shark

bugs

2 Watch the film. Tick the right answers.

V 11

Sieh dir den Film an. Setze Häkchen bei den richtigen Antworten.

1. Who's visiting the Everglades? ☐ Grace ☐ Cedric
2. Who takes them on the fishing trip? ☐ Uncle Ray ☐ a guide
3. What does Grace like about the trip? ☐ the bugs ☐ the boat ride
4. At what age do you need a fishing license? ☐ 15 years ☐ 16 years
5. How many guides are in the Everglades? ☐ over 400 ☐ over 300
6. What animal do they see in the water? ☐ a snake ☐ a shark

3 Collect information about one of the animals. Make a fact card.

Sammelt Informationen über eins der Tiere. Erstellt einen Steckbrief.

alligator shark snake

Animal:

Where it lives:

What it eats:

How old it can get:

Other facts:

✓ Ich kann einen Naturfilm verstehen.

An exciting future

1 Read the texts. Lies die Texte. ► Vokabeln S.130 (V11)

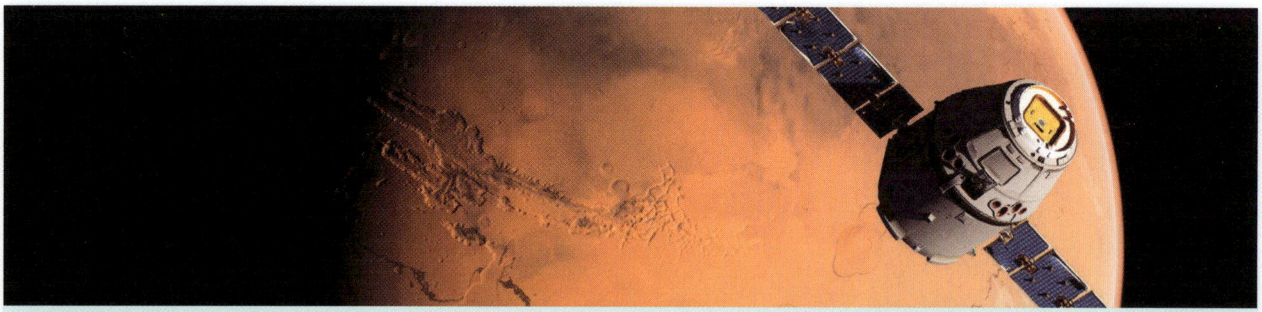

FUTURE DIRECTIONS

How will technology change our lives in the future? *The Miami News* is looking at this question during May. We've written about food and farming and artificial intelligence. But Florida has always been important for space travel, and last week we wrote about the topic 'Our future is on Mars'. Here are some of the letters and emails we received.

Dear Editor,
I'm writing about the topic 'Our future is on Mars'. In my opinion, having a human colony on Mars would be a good idea. For one thing, a war or another disaster could destroy life on Earth. Having a second home on Mars could help us survive.
I also think that humans could start again on Mars. We could build a better, happier, and more peaceful future for everyone.
For all these reasons, I think we should have a colony on Mars.
Sincerely,
Delvon Andrews
Orlando, Florida

Dear Editor,
I'm a high school student who worries about the future of our planet. I don't think it's a good idea to live on Mars.
Firstly, Mars has more extreme temperatures than Earth, and there wouldn't be enough air, water, and food.
Secondly, Mars is a long way away. Sending more than four or five people would be too expensive.
I believe it's wrong to move to Mars. We should try to save our planet and build a better future on Earth.
Sincerely,
Cassidy Rogers
Tampa, Florida

2 Match the words with their definitions.

Verbinde die Wörter mit ihren Definitionen.

1. disaster  2. destroy  3. survive  4. enough 

break something | not too much, not too little | a very bad event | not die

3 Are you for or against a future on Mars? Talk to a partner. ► Vokabeln S. 129 (V10)

Bist du für oder gegen eine Zukunft auf dem Mars? Sprecht miteinander.

Du kannst auch Argumente aus dem Text gegenüber benutzen.

Mars could be a second home | there wouldn't be enough food | …

A In my opinion, a future on Mars is a good/bad idea. For one thing we could survive on Mars. I also think that … .

B I agree./I don't agree. The temperatures there are too extreme. … .

4 Put the words in the right group.

Schreibe die Wörter in die richtige Gruppe.

artificial meat | the Moon ✓ | drones | air taxis | robot nurses | the solar system | cars without drivers | other planets

A  Space	B  Transport	C  Food and health
the Moon		

5 Read the poem. Tick the right answers.

A 19

Lies das Gedicht. Setze Häkchen bei den richtigen Antworten.

In the near future, cars will fly.
I will have to navigate[1] my way through the sky.
This is my prediction[2] for you and me –
A world of possibilities[3], just wait and see.

We'll travel to the Moon, build a home on Mars,
But we won't get a suntan if we go that far!
This is my prediction for you and me –
A world of possibilities, just wait and see.

The future is exciting, in a very special way[4],
But will it be better than the life we live today?
This is my question for you and me –
A world of possibilities? Let's wait and see.

1 to navigate – *steuern*; 2 prediction – *die Vorhersage*; 3 possibilities – *Möglichkeiten*;
4 in a very special way – *auf eine ganz besondere Weise*

1. What does the speaker think will happen in the future?
   There's more than one right answer.

   ☐ People will drive in the sky. ☐ People will swim to Mars.

   ☐ Space travel will be possible. ☐ The future will be boring.

2. Why won't we get a suntan?

   ☐ Mars is too cold. ☐ Mars is too far away from the sun.

3. Does the speaker think the future will be good or bad?

   ☐ good ☐ bad ☐ They are not sure.

6 Practise reading the poem. Perform it in class.

Übt, das Gedicht zu lesen. Tragt es in der Klasse vor.

Language

Wenn du eine **Person** genauer beschreiben möchtest, verwendest du **who**.
Bei einer **Sache** verwendest du **which**.

A vegetarian is **someone who** doesn't eat meat.
Artificial meat is **a kind of meat which** doesn't come from animals.

7 Circle the right word. Kreise das richtige Wort ein.

1. This is the spacecraft **which** | **who** will take tourists into space.
2. The person **who** | **which** writes the best letter will win the competition.
4. These are the drones **which** | **who** can fly at 50 km/h.
5. This is the chef **which** | **that** cooks dishes with insects.

8 Put the words in the right order.

Bringe die Wörter in die richtige Reihenfolge.

1. which | was the spacecraft | The Vostok 3KA | took the first human into space.

   The Vostok 3KA was the spacecraft

2. first stood on the Moon. | was the astronaut | who | Neil Armstrong

3. The Model T | which | was a car | was very popular in the 1920s.

4. wrote a computer program. | Ada Lovelace was a scientist | who

9 **Your turn:** A comment

Write a comment about a possible future development.

Schreibe einen Kommentar über eine mögliche Entwicklung in der Zukunft.

► Vokabeln S. 129 (V10)

Step 1: Choose one of the statements. Wähle eine der Aussagen aus.

A. Living on the Moon is a **good** idea.

B. Living on the Moon is a **bad** idea.

C. It would be **great** to have robot nurses in hospitals.

D. It would **not** be great to have robot nurses in hospitals.

Step 2: Collect arguments for your statement.
Sammle Argumente für deine Aussage.

C. It would be great to have robot nurses in hospitals:
- *not enough staff*
- *cheaper than real nurses*
- *help people with daily routines*
- *...*

Step 3: Choose two arguments from your notes and add examples.
Wähle zwei Argumente aus deinen Notizen aus und füge Beispiele hinzu.

- *not enough staff: hospital in Ravensburg needs 77 more nurses, ...*
- *help people with daily routines: to get dressed, to feed them, ...*

Step 4: Write your comment.
Use this structure:
- Introduction (Einleitung)
- Your opinion (deine Meinung)
- Arguments and examples (Argumente und Beispiele)
- Conclusion (Schlusswort)

People already use robots, for example, to clean the house. I think that robots could also be useful in hospitals. It would be great to have robot nurses. Firstly, hospitals do not have enough staff. For example, ... Secondly, ... For all these reasons, I think ... .

✓ Ich kann meine Meinung äußern.

Celebrating life in New Orleans

1 Match the words with the photos. Ordne die Wörter den Bildern zu.

coffin | cemetery ✓ | to march | funeral

A

B

C
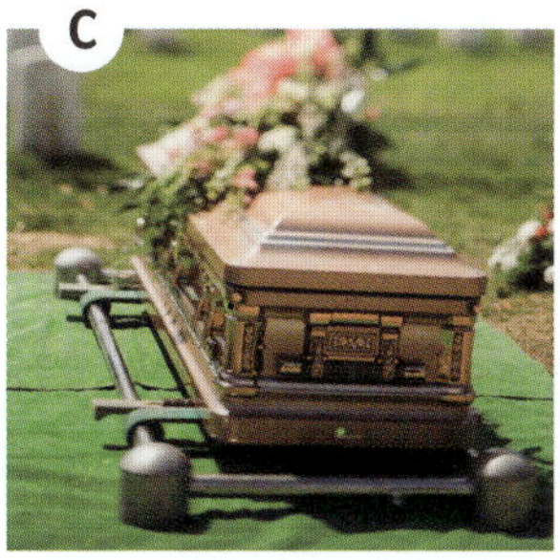
D

cemetery ______ ______ ______

2 Jazz funerals

A 20 **a)** Listen to the radio feature.
Which three things do they talk about?
Höre dir das Radio-Feature an.
Über welche drei Dinge reden sie?

- [ ] clothes
- [ ] food
- [ ] music
- [ ] a terrible storm

A 20 **b)** Listen again and complete the notes.
Höre noch einmal zu und vervollständige die Notizen.

1. Who takes part in a jazz funeral?

   family, friends and ______

2. What is special about jazz funerals?

   In the second part of the funeral, you can hear ______
   ______ *and people* ______

3. What information do you hear about Hurricane Katrina?

   It happened in ______ *and about* ______

Culture
New Orleans gilt als die Heimat der Jazz-Musik. Auch Musikstile wie Gospel und Blues werden dort viel gespielt. Die Stadt hat viele Musikclubs.

✓ Ich kann ein Radio-Feature verstehen.

Civil rights and the South

1 Look at the photos. What do they tell you?

Sieh dir die Fotos an. Was sagen sie dir?

A

In the 1960s

B

2009–2017

C

In the 2020s

2 Read the texts. Lies dir die Texte durch.

A 21

INTRODUCTION

Slavery ended in 1865, but new laws in the late 19th and early 20th century led to segregation: Black and white people weren't allowed to go to the same schools. On trains and buses, they had to sit in different seats. Often, Black people weren't allowed to vote either. These laws were the reason why the civil rights movement started in 1954.

A 22

A MONTGOMERY, ALABAMA

On December 1, 1955, Rosa Parks got on a bus and sat down on a free seat. When the bus driver asked her to move so a white person could sit down, she didn't. The police arrested her, and she had to pay $14. When people heard of this, they stopped using public buses in Montgomery. The boycott lasted a year and, finally, they changed the law.

A police photo of Rosa Parks

The National Civil Rights Museum in Memphis

A 23

B LITTLE ROCK, ARKANSAS

In 1954, the US Supreme Court[1] decided that segregation at schools was not allowed anymore.
In September 1957, the first Black students went to the all-white Little Rock Central High School.
But many local people tried to stop them from going inside.
The US president ordered[2] the Arkansas National Guard[3] to protect the students. Lots of people shouted at the students as they walked into school.

A protesting crowd

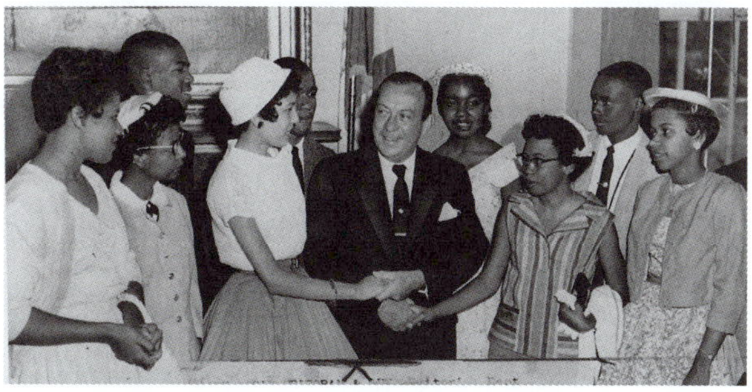
Mayor of New York City with the teenagers from Central High School

A 24

C BIRMINGHAM, ALABAMA

In the early 1960s, Birmingham was one of the most divided cities in the country. Although the city had a 40 % Black population, it had no Black police officers or bus drivers, for example. In 1963 James Bevel, Martin Luther King and others wanted to change this. They organized boycotts of stores, restaurants, and other public places. James Bevel asked students to peacefully protest. But the police hit Black children as they walked to the mayor's office.

Protests at Graymont Elementary School

Foot Soldiers statue in Kelly Ingram Park

1 US Supreme Court – *der Oberste Gerichtshof der USA*; 2 to order – *befehlen*;
3 National Guard – *die Nationalgarde; unterstützt das Militär innerhalb eines Bundesstaats*

A 25

D MEMPHIS, TENNESSEE

In April 1968, Martin Luther King was in Memphis to support a strike by Black public workers. On April 3, King gave a famous speech there. The next evening King was shot on a balcony of the Lorraine Motel. His death caused riots all over the country. About 100,000 people watched King's funeral in Atlanta, Georgia. At the end, they sang the song 'We Shall Overcome'.

The Lorraine Motel, Memphis

Dr. Martin Luther King

3 Read the introduction again and circle the right words.

Lies die Einführung nochmal und kreise die richtigen Wörter ein.

1. In 1865 slavery **ended** | **started**.
2. Black and white people still had to **go to different schools** | **eat different food**. They had to use different **trains** | **seats** too.
3. This was called **protesting** | **segregation**.
4. The civil rights movement started in **the 1800s** | **1954**.

4 Home group and expert group.

a) Home group: Get into groups of 4. Each of you chooses one of the texts.

Heimgruppe: Bildet Vierergruppen. Jeder von euch wählt einen Text aus.

b) Read your text and answer the questions on the next page. Take notes.

Lies deinen Text und beantworte die Fragen auf der nächsten Seite. Mache dir Notizen.

1. What happened? Underline key words and phrases in your text.
2. When did it happen? Underline the right date in your text.
3. What was the message?

4. Were the people **successful**?

c) Expert group: Find students who have read the same text as you. Compare your notes.
Expertengruppe: Finde Schülerinnen und Schüler, die denselben Text gelesen haben, wie du. Vergleicht eure Notizen.

Group A: Montgomery, Alabama
Group B: Little Rock, Arkansas
Group C: Birmingham, Alabama
Group D: Memphis, Tennessee

d) Meet your home group again. Present what you have found out. Take notes about the other texts.
Geht wieder zu eurer Heimgruppe. Präsentiert eure Ergebnisse.
Macht euch Notizen zu den anderen Texten.

5 Go online. Watch and listen to 'I have a dream' by Martin Luther King. Then answer the questions.
Schaut und hört euch im Internet 'I have a dream' von Martin Luther King an. Dann beantwortet die Fragen. ► Vokabeln S.123 (V2)

1. What and who can you see?

I can see

2. How does it make you feel?

I feel

✓ Ich kann einen Artikel aus einem Geschichtsmagazin verstehen.

Checklist

Complete the sentences.

Vervollständige die Sätze.

must take | can't walk ✓ | must take | may take | can't hang out | mustn't play | may stay

1. Nick has broken his leg. He *can't walk* __________ to school. His dad __________ him there by car.

A
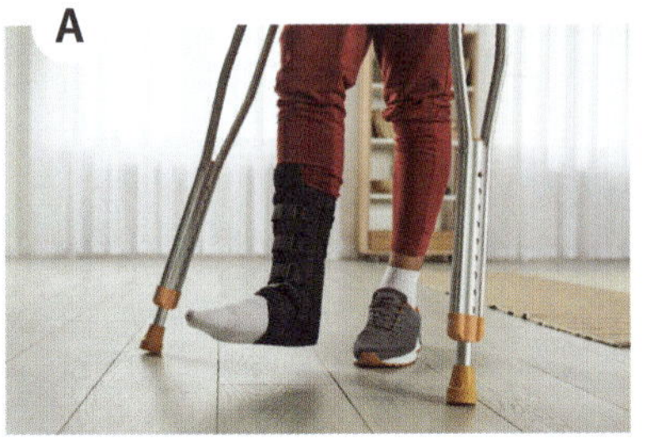

2. This is the public park in our town. It's nice, but we __________ football there.

B

3. Sarah invited me to her birthday party next weekend. She said that Macy and I __________ there until Sunday.

C

4. My parents are looking for a holiday cottage near the sea. I __________ a friend. That's great!

D

5. I'm sorry, we __________ today. Our neighbour is ill, so I __________ __________ her dog for a walk.

E

Task: A multimedia presentation

Give a multimedia presentation about your dream for a better future.

Haltet eine Multimedia-Präsentation über euren Traum von einer besseren Zukunft.

Step 1: Collect ideas.
Sammelt Ideen.

no racism/discrimination, peace, protecting animals, fair trade, ...

Step 2: Choose one idea. Think of three aspects of your dream. Find one example for each aspect.
Sucht eine Idee aus. Überlegt euch drei Punkte eures Traums. Findet für jeden Punkt ein Beispiel.

Protecting animals

1. *Farm animals must have better lives. Example: cows are kept outside, eat grass*
2. *People should eat less meat. Example: an influencer who became a vegetarian.*
3. *People must treat their pets well. Example: ...*

Step 3: Illustrate each aspect with a link to an audio or video, a photo or a diagram.
Veranschaulicht jeden Punkt mit einem Link zu einem Audio oder Video, einem Foto oder einem Diagramm.

Media tip
Mit Audios, Videos und Fotos kannst du Gefühle erzeugen. Diagramme können Fakten anschaulich darstellen.

Step 4: Write an introduction and a conclusion. Say what your dream is and why it's important to you.
Schreibt eine Einleitung und ein Fazit. Sagt, was euer Traum ist und warum er euch wichtig ist.

Our dream for a better future is a world in which animals are protected. We should do a lot to improve their lives. ...
Protecting animals is very important to us because ... .
Help us to make a better future for animals.

Music from the South

1 What kinds of music do you think these musicians play or played?

Was glaubst du, was für Musik diese Musiker spielen oder gespielt haben?

1 Louis Armstrong (1901–1971) sang and played the cornet[1] as a young boy in New Orleans. In the 1920s he moved to Chicago and became one of the best trumpeters[2] there. As a singer, his most famous hit was 'What a Wonderful World'.

1 cornet – *das Kornett (Musikinstrument)*
2 trumpeter – *der Trompeter / die Trompeterin*

2 Elvis Presley (1935–1977), was born in Mississippi. Elvis had many hits in the 1950s, including 'Jailhouse[3] Rock'. In the 1960s he became an actor, but in 1968 he returned to music. He died nine years later. Elvis is also known as 'the king of rock and roll'.

3 jailhouse – *das Gefängnis*

3 Tina Turner (1939–2023)
was born in Tennessee.
In the first part of her career[4], she performed[5] with her husband, Ike Turner. But in 1976 Tina left Ike. In the 1980s she was very successful alone with hits like 'What's Love Got To Do With It'.

4 career – *die Karriere*
5 to perform – *auftreten, aufführen*

4 Taylor Swift (born 1989)
is from Pennsylvania, but she moved to Nashville with her family as a teenager. Taylor started her career as a country singer, but her later songs like 'Shake It Off' are more influenced by pop and dance.

2 Listen online to one of the songs in the text. Talk about the song.

Hört euch online einen der Songs aus dem Text an. Sprecht über den Song.

slow | fast | different | old | modern | OK | …

excited | tired | like I want to dance | sad | happy | …

A What do you think of …? How does it make you feel?

B I really like / don't like it because it's … . It makes me feel … .

Words and pictures

1 Write the right words under each photo.

Schreibe die richtigen Wörter unter die Fotos.

barbecue | humans | carnival | strike | hurricane | wetlands ✓ | Chinese | person

A

w	e	t	l	a	n	d (1)	s

B

		(2)			(3)	

C

(4)		(5)		(6)			

D

		(7)			

E

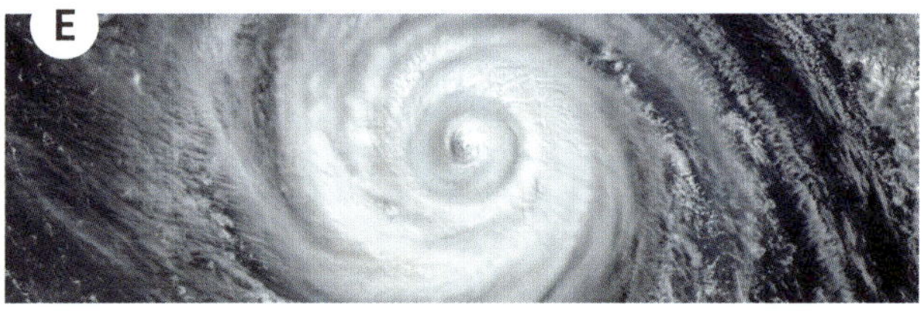

				(8)			(9)	

F

	(10)						

G

	(11)		(12)		

H

				(13)	(14)	of colour

2 Complete the sentence with the letters in the grey boxes.

Vervollständige den Satz mit den Buchstaben aus den grauen Kästchen.

Don't treat a person unfairly because of what they look like or who they are.

That's	d														.
	1	2	3	4	5	6	7	8	9	10	11	12	13	14	

Unit quiz

1 What are the right endings for the sentences? Tick.

Wie lauten die richtigen Satzenden? Setze Häkchen.

1. Jacksonville is the biggest city in the South with about …
   - **n** ☑ 970,000 people.
   - **s** ☐ 9,700,000 people.
2. Cape Canaveral is a …
   - **L** ☐ famous festival in Florida.
   - **M** ☐ launch site in Florida.
3. Hurricanes often hit the …
   - **e** ☐ coast of the South.
   - **o** ☐ Everglades.
4. The Everglades are an area with …
   - **u** ☐ mountains and animal farms.
   - **m** ☐ forests and lakes.
5. The guides in the Everglades …
   - **p** ☐ teach visitors respect.
   - **s** ☐ show how to catch a shark.
6. New Orleans is famous for …
   - **h** ☐ jazz music.
   - **a** ☐ French food.
7. In the 1950s and 1960s, Black people protested against …
   - **t** ☐ US space missions.
   - **i** ☐ racism and segregation.
8. Martin Luther King and James Bevel …
   - **s** ☐ organised peaceful protests.
   - **a** ☐ fought for discrimination.

2 Complete the sentence with the letters in front of the right facts.

Vervollständige den Satz mit den Buchstaben vor den richtigen Fakten.

In April 1968, Martin Luther King was shot after a famous speech

i	*n*								
	1	2	3	4	5	6	7	8	.

V1 Parts of a building Teile eines Gebäudes

1

balcony
der Balkon

2

door
die Tür

3

floor
der Fußboden

4

elevator (AE),
lift (BE)
der Aufzug

5

ground level
das Erdgeschoss

6

solar panel
der Sonnen-
kollektor

7

story (AE),
floor (BE)
die Etage;
das Stockwerk

8

entrance
der Eingang

9
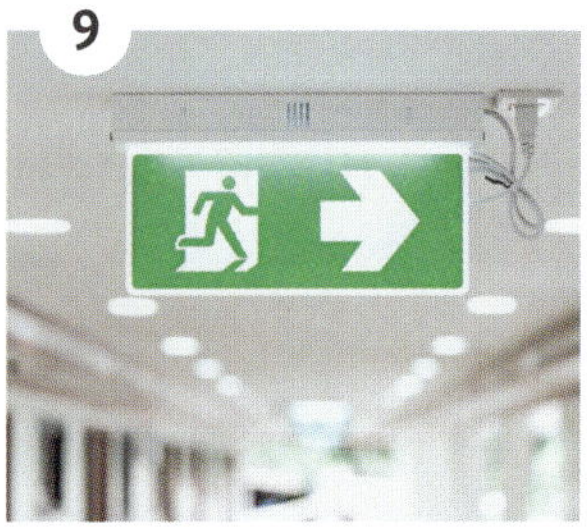
exit
der Ausgang

10

roof
das Dach

11

room
das Zimmer;
der Raum

12

stairs
die Treppe

13

wall
die Wand

14

window
das Fenster

V2 Adjectives Adjektive

1

awesome
super; spitze
exciting
aufregend
fantastic
fantastisch, großartig
wonderful
wunderbar

2

awful
schrecklich; furchtbar
bad
schlecht, schlimm
terrible
furchtbar; schlimm; schrecklich

3

friendly
freundlich
great
toll
happy
glücklich
nice
nett; schön

4

crazy
verrückt

5

sad
traurig
unhappy
unglücklich

6

interesting
interessant
nosy
neugierig

7

bored
gelangweilt
strange
seltsam; merkwürdig
unusual
ungewöhnlich

V3 School life in the USA Schulleben in den USA

1

cafeteria
die Cafeteria; die Mensa

2

detention
das Nachsitzen

3

drama
Theater

4

dress code
die Kleiderordnung

5

exchange student
der Austauschschüler

6

film production
die Filmproduktion

7

football game
das Footballspiel

8

homeroom (AE)
Treffen vor der ersten Stunde

9

locker
das Schließfach

10

metal detector
der Metalldetektor

11

Pledge of Allegiance
der Treueeid

12

practice
die Probe; das Training

13

schedule
der Stundenplan

14

school bus
der Schulbus

15

student council
der Schülerrat

16

yearbook
das Jahrbuch

V4 Celebrating special days Besondere Tage feiern

1

to dance
tanzen

2

to eat cookies
Kekse essen

3

to play games
Spiele spielen

4

to light a candle
eine Kerze anzünden

5

to have a special meal
eine besondere Mahlzeit essen

6

to prepare a meal
eine Mahlzeit vorbereiten

7

to make a video call
einen Videoanruf machen

8

to put up decorations
Dekoration aufhängen

9

to take part in a parade
an einer Parade teilnehmen
to watch a parade
eine Parade anschauen

10

to give or receive presents
Geschenke geben oder bekommen

11

to pick someone up
jemanden abholen
to visit the family
die Familie besuchen

12

to wear special clothes
besondere Kleidung tragen

V5 Life cycle of a product Lebenszyklus eines Produkts

1

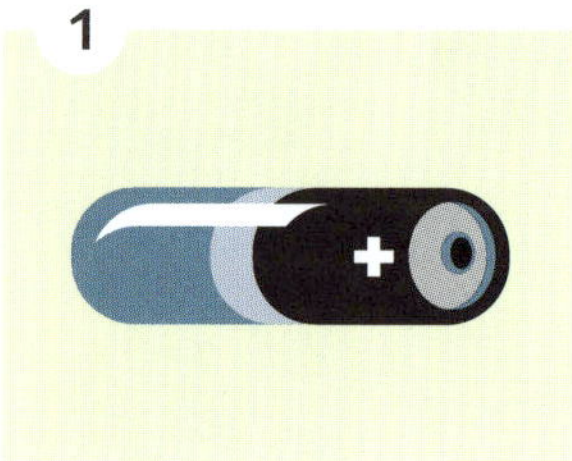

battery
der Akku;
die Batterie

2

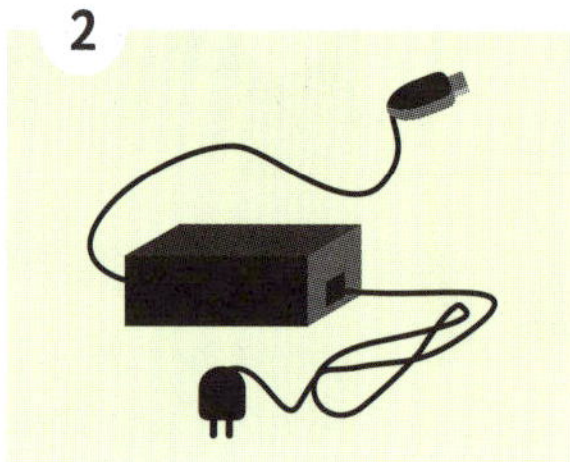

to charge
aufladen; laden

3

to check
überprüfen;
kontrollieren

4

to dispose of
entsorgen

5

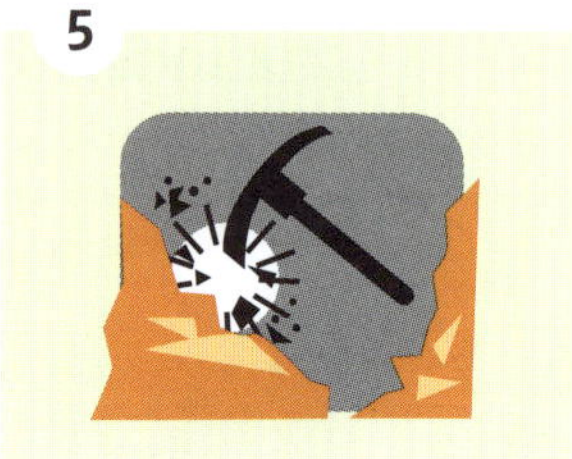

to mine
abbauen

6

to process
verarbeiten;
aufbereiten

7

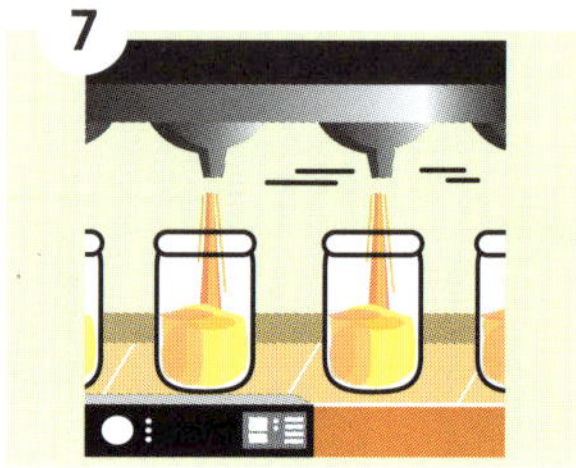

to produce
herstellen;
produzieren

8

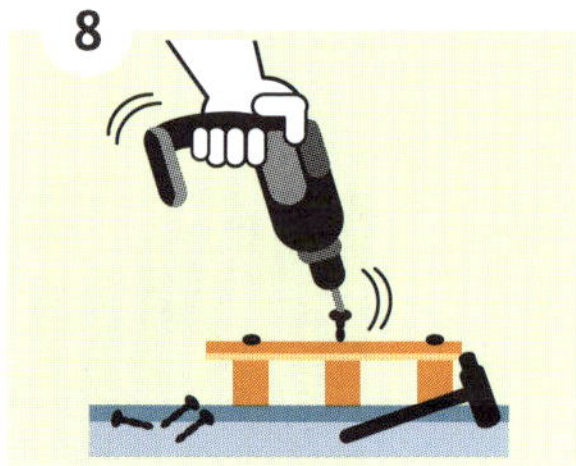

to put together
zusammenbauen

9

device
das Gerät
to program
programmieren

10

to package
verpacken
packaging
die Verpackung

11

to recycle
recyceln; wieder-
verwenden

12

to deliver
liefern
to transport
transportieren

13

to reduce
reduzieren;
verringern

14

waste
der Abfall

V6 Social work Soziale Arbeit

1

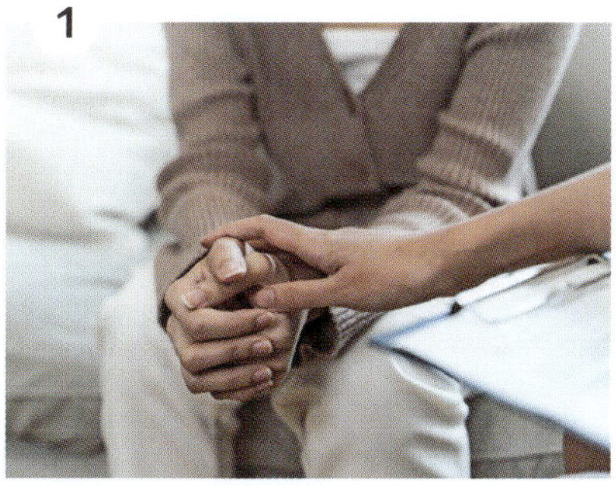

advice der Rat
to cope bewältigen
solution die Lösung

2

alcohol der Alkohol
drug die Droge

3

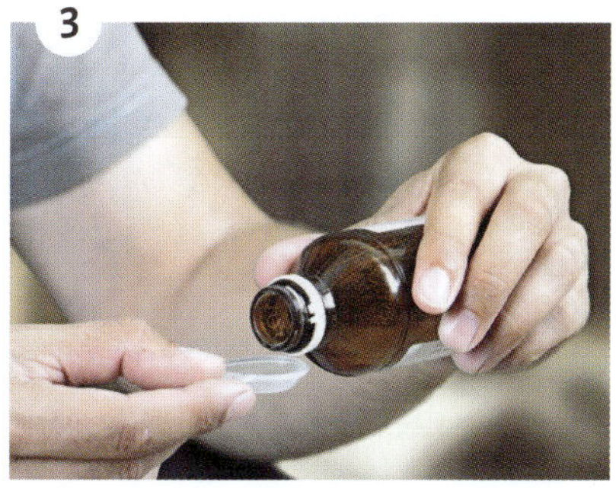

health die Gesundheit
ill krank
medicine die Medizin

4

homeless obdachlos
jobless arbeitslos
to offer anbieten

5

outreach centre
die Beratungsstelle
practical help
die praktische Hilfe

6

to get into debt
sich verschulden
to pay rent
Miete zahlen

V7 Describing a role model Ein Vorbild beschreiben

to achieve one's goals
seine Ziele erreichen
ambitious
ehrgeizig
confident
selbstsicher; selbstbewusst
to encourage
ermutigen; unterstützen
to inspire
inspirieren

to never give up nie aufgeben
patient geduldig
strong stark
successful erfolgreich
talented talentiert

V8 Infrastructure and services Infrastruktur und Dienstleistungen

1

airport
der Flughafen

2
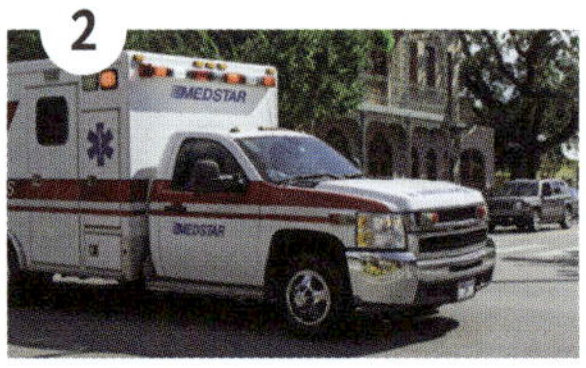
ambulance
der Kranken-wagen

3

bank
die Bank

4

bus station
die Bushaltestelle

5

café
das Café

6

gym
das Fitnessstudio

7

hairdresser's
der Friseursalon

8
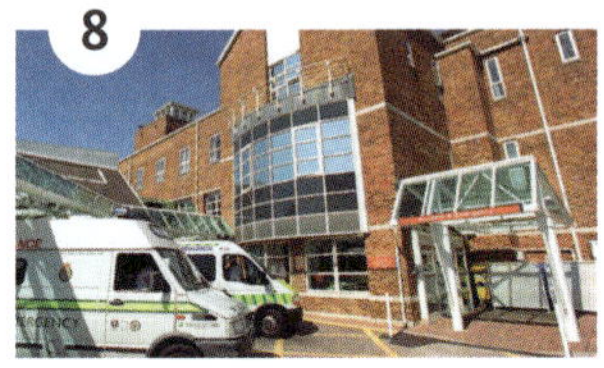
hospital
das Krankenhaus

9

hotel
das Hotel

10

library
die Bibliothek

11

museum
das Museum

12

park
der Park

13

playground
der Spielplatz

14

police station
das Polizeirevier

15

sidewalk
der Gehweg

16

store (AE);
shop (BE)
das Geschäft

17

town hall
das Rathaus

18

train station
der Bahnhof

19

transport
Verkehrsmittel; Beförderung

20

subway (AE);
underground (BE)
die U-Bahn

V9 Attitudes and behaviour Einstellungen und Verhalten

1

to accept – akzeptieren
to agree – zustimmen
to be allowed – dürfen
to respect – respektieren

2

civil rights – Bürgerrechte
to organise – organisieren
to protest – protestieren
to stop – aufhalten; verhindern

3
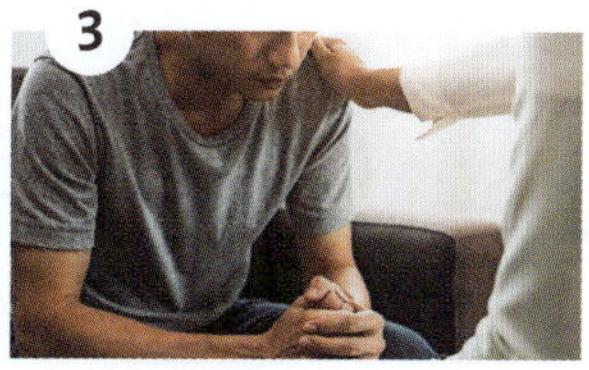

to cope with – fertig werden mit; bewältigen
to take seriously – ernst nehmen
to treat – behandeln
to understand – verstehen

4

to discriminate against – benachteiligen
discrimination – Diskriminierung
equal – gleichberechtigt; gleich
racism – der Rassismus

V10 Giving opinions Meinungen äußern

Introducing your opinion Deine Meinung einleiten

1	I agree	ich stimme zu
2	I believe	ich glaube
3	I'm sure	ich bin mir sicher
4	I think	ich denke
5	in my opinion,	meiner Meinung nach

Structuring what you say Strukturieren, was du sagst

6	again	nochmal; wieder
7	also	auch
8	although	obwohl
9	firstly, secondly,	erstens, zweitens
10	because of	wegen
11	that's why	deswegen
12	for all these reasons,	aus all diesen Gründen

So kannst du Sätze anfangen, in denen du deine Meinung sagst.

Wenn du diese Wörter benutzt, dann wirkst du überzeugender und die Menschen können besser verstehen, was du sagen willst.

V11 In the future In der Zukunft

1

astronaut
der Astronaut / die Astronautin

2

to destroy
zerstören

3

disaster
die Katastrophe

4
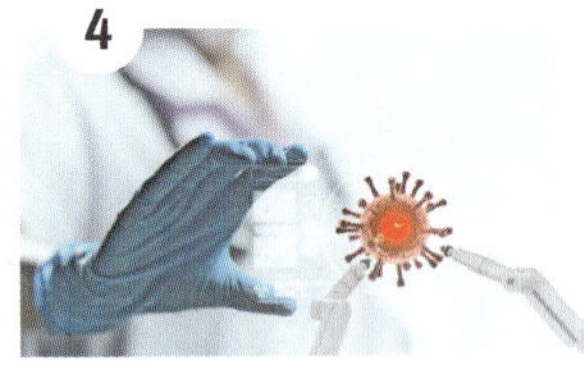
disease
die Krankheit

5

drone
die Drohne

6

Earth
die Erde

7

environment
die Umwelt

8

peace
der Frieden

9

planet
der Planet

10

to protect
beschützen

11

to save
retten; sparen; speichern

12

scientist
der Wissenschaftler / die Wissenschaftlerin

13

solar system
das Sonnensystem

14

solution
die Lösung

15

space
der Weltraum

16

spacecraft
das Raumschiff

17

to survive
überleben

18

sustainable
nachhaltig

19
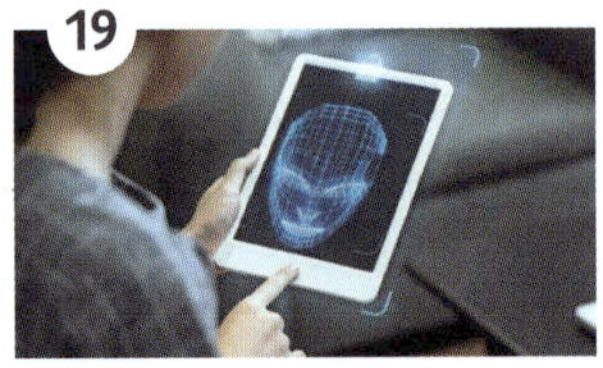
technology
die Technologie

20

war
der Krieg

A

a	ein/eine
a few	ein paar; wenige; einige
a lot	viel
a lot of	viel(e); eine Menge
a piece of	eine Scheibe; ein Stück
a while	eine Weile
a bit	ein bisschen; ein wenig
a.m.	vormittags *(Uhrzeit)*
about	über; ungefähr
above	über; oberhalb
to **accept**	annehmen; hinnehmen; akzeptieren
accident	Unfall
account	Konto
to **achieve**	erreichen; schaffen; leisten
acre	Acre (Flächenmaß: 4.050 m²)
across	über; quer durch; hinüber
to **act**	spielen; sich verhalten; handeln
activity	Aktivität
actor	Schauspieler/ Schauspielerin
ad	Werbung; Anzeige
AD (= **Anno Domini**)	nach Christus
to **add**	hinzufügen; ergänzen; addieren
adult	Erwachsener/ Erwachsene
adventure	Abenteuer
advice	Rat; Ratschlag
afraid	ängstlich
Africa	Afrika
African	afrikanisch; aus Afrika; Afrikaner/Afrikanerin
African American	afroamerikanisch; Afroamerikaner/ Afroamerikanerin
after	nach; danach; nachdem; später
afternoon	Nachmittag
again	noch einmal; wieder
against	gegen
age	Alter
ago	vor *(zeitlich)*
to **agree (on sth)**	sich (auf etw.) einigen; (etw.) zustimmen
agreement	Einigung; Zustimmung; Vereinbarung
air	Luft
airport	Flughafen
alarm	Wecker; Alarm
alcohol	Alkohol
alive	am Leben
all	alle; alles; ganz
allergic to	allergisch gegen
allergy	Allergie
alligator	Alligator
almost	fast; beinahe
alone	allein
along	entlang
already	schon; bereits
also	auch
although	obwohl
always	immer
amazing	unglaublich; toll
ambitious	ehrgeizig
ambulance	Krankenwagen; Rettungswagen
America	Amerika
American	amerikanisch; aus Amerika; Amerikaner/ Amerikanerin
American football	American Football
Amish	amisch
an	ein/eine
ancestor	Vorfahre/Vorfahrin
and	und
Anglo-Saxon	angelsächsisch; Angelsachse/ Angelsächsin
angry	wütend; böse
animal	Tier
animal home	Tierheim
ankle	Fußgelenk; Fußknöchel
announcement	Durchsage; Ankündigung
another	ein anderer / eine andere; noch ein; weitere
answer	Antwort
to **answer**	beantworten; antworten
anti-	Anti-; Nicht-

any	irgendwelche
anything	irgendetwas
Anything else?	Darf es sonst noch etwas sein?
anyway	wie auch immer; trotzdem; jedenfalls; sowieso
anywhere	irgendwo
apartment ***(AE)***	Wohnung
app	App; Anwendung
apple	Apfel
apprenticeship	Ausbildung; Lehre
April	April
aquarium	Aquarium
Arabic	Arabisch; arabisch
area	Gegend; Gebiet; Fläche
argument	Argument; Streit; Auseinandersetzung
arm	Arm
army	Armee; Heer
around	rund um; um ... herum; ungefähr (um)
to **arrest**	festnehmen; verhaften
to **arrive**	ankommen
arrow	Pfeil
art	Kunst
article	Artikel; Bericht
artificial	künstlich
artificial intelligence (AI)	künstliche Intelligenz (KI)
arts	Kunst
as ... as	so ... wie
Asian	asiatisch; aus Asien; Asiate/Asiatin
to **ask**	fragen
to **ask sb on a date**	jdn. um ein Date bitten
to **ask for**	bitten um; fragen nach
assessment	Begutachtung; Beurteilung
assistant	Verkäufer/Verkäuferin
astronaut	Astronaut/Astronautin
at	in; an; um; bei; auf
at first	zuerst; zunächst
at home	zu Hause
at least	mindestens; wenigstens; immerhin
at night	nachts
at the moment	gerade; im Moment
at the top	oben
ate	aß
athlete	Athlet/Athletin; Leichtathlet/Leichtathletin
attack	Anschlag; Angriff
to **attend**	teilnehmen (an); besuchen
August	August
aunt	Tante
Australia	Australien
autumn	Herbst
average	Durchschnitts-; durchschnittlich
awake	bei Bewusstsein; wach
award	Preis; Auszeichnung
away	weg; entfernt
awesome	super; spitze
awful	schrecklich; furchtbar

B

B&B (bed and breakfast)	Frühstückspension
babysitting	Babysitten
back	zurück; Rücken; Rückseite
background	Hintergrund; Herkunft
bad	schlecht; böse; schlimm
bag	Tasche; Tüte
bagpipes	Dudelsack
to **bake**	backen
balcony	Balkon
ball	Ball; Kugel
banana	Banane
band	Band; Musikgruppe
bank	(Finanz-)Bank
bar	Tafel; Riegel
barbecue	Grillfest; Grillen
to **bark**	bellen
baseball	Baseball
basketball	Basketball
bathroom	Badezimmer; Bad
battery	Akku; Batterie
BC (= before Christ)	vor Christus
to **be**	sein

to **be able (to do sth)**	(etw. tun) können; (etw. tun) dürfen
to **be allowed (to do sth)**	(etw. tun) dürfen
to **be ashamed of**	sich schämen für/ wegen
to **be born**	geboren werden
to **be fun**	Spaß machen
to **be going on**	los sein
to **be going to do sth**	etw. tun werden
to **be good at**	gut sein in
to **be homesick**	Heimweh haben
to **be in pain**	Schmerzen haben
to **be interested in**	sich interessieren für
to **be prepared**	vorbereitet sein
to **be right**	recht haben
to **be sorry**	leidtun
to **be wrong**	nicht stimmen; unrecht haben; sich irren
been	gewesen
beach	Strand
beam	Balken; Strahl
bear	Bär
beautiful	schön; hübsch
became	wurde
because	da; weil
because of	wegen
become, become	werden, geworden
bed	Bett
bedroom	Schlafzimmer; Kinderzimmer
bee	Biene
before	vor; vorher; zuvor; bevor
began	begann; fing an
begin	beginnen; anfangen
begun	begonnen; angefangen
behind	hinter
to **believe**	glauben
bell	Glocke
bench	Bank; Sitzbank
best	beste/bester/bestes
better	besser
between	zwischen
big	groß
bike	Fahrrad
biker	Fahrradfahrer/ Fahrradfahrerin; Motorradfahrer/ Motorradfahrerin
bin	Mülleimer
biology	Biologie
bionic	bionisch
bird	Vogel
birthday	Geburtstag
biscuit	Keks
bison	Bison
Black	schwarz *(soziale Kategorie)*
blog	Blog
blood	Blut
board	Tafel
boarding	Einsteigen
boat	Boot
book	Buch; Heft
to **book**	buchen; reservieren
boot	Stiefel
bored	gelangweilt
boring	langweilig
to **borrow**	ausleihen
boss	Chef/Chefin
both ... and ...	sowohl ... als auch ...
bottle	Flasche
bought, bought	kaufte, gekauft
box	Box; Kiste; Schachtel
boy	Junge
boycott	Boykott
brave	mutig; tapfer
bread	Brot
break	Pause
to **break**	brechen; zerbrechen
breakfast	Frühstück
to **breathe**	atmen
bridge	Brücke
brilliant	toll
to **bring**	(mit)bringen
Britain	Großbritannien
British	britisch
broke	brach, zerbrach
broken	gebrochen; zerbrochen; kaputt
brother	Bruder
brought	brachte (mit)

brown	braun
brush	Bürste; Pinsel
to **brush**	putzen; bürsten
to **brush one's teeth**	sich die Zähne putzen
bug	Insekt; Käfer
to **build**	bauen
building	Gebäude
built, built	baute, gebaut
bullying	Mobbing; Schikanieren; Tyrannisieren
burger	Hamburger
to **burn**	brennen, verbrennen
burnt, burnt	brannte, gebrannt; verbrannte, verbrannt
bus	Bus
bus stop	Bushaltestelle
business	Unternehmen; Geschäft; Branche
busy	beschäftigt; belebt; voller Menschen
but	aber
butterfly	Schmetterling
button	Knopf; Taste
to **buy**	kaufen
by	von; an; neben
by (bike)	mit (dem Fahrrad)
Bye.	Tschüss.

C

cabbage	Kohl; Kraut
caber	Baumstamm
caber toss	Baumstammwerfen
cabin	Kabine
cable car	Seilbahn
café	Café
cafeteria	Cafeteria; Mensa
cake	Kuchen
calf	Kalb
call	Anruf; Ruf; Gespräch
to **call**	rufen; anrufen; nennen
calm	ruhig; friedlich
to **calm down**	sich beruhigen
came	kam
camera	Kamera; Fotoapparat
camp	Camp; Lager
camping	Camping; Zelten
campsite	Campingplatz; Zeltplatz
can	können
Canada	Kanada
canal	Kanal
cancelled	abgesagt
candle	Kerze
canyon	Schlucht; Canyon
cap	Mütze; Kappe
capital (city)	Hauptstadt
captain	Kapitän/Kapitänin
car	Auto
car boot sale	Flohmarkt *(Verkauf aus dem Kofferraum)*
car park	Parkplatz
card	Pappe; Karton; Karte
careful	vorsichtig
carnival	Karneval; Fasching
carpenter	Tischler/Tischlerin; Zimmerer/Zimmerin
carrot	Karotte
to **carry**	tragen; befördern
cartoon	Cartoon
castle	Schloss; Burg
cat	Katze
to **catch**	fangen
cathedral	Dom; Kathedrale
Catholic	Katholik/Katholikin; katholisch
cattle	Rinder; Vieh
to **cause**	verursachen
caught, caught	fing, gefangen
cave	Höhle
to **celebrate**	feiern
celebration	Feier; Fest
Celt	Kelte/Keltin
cemetery	Friedhof
center ***(AE)***, **centre** ***(BE)***	Zentrum; Mitte; Center
Central Europe	Mitteleuropa
century	Jahrhundert
cereal	Müsli
certain	bestimmte/ bestimmter/ bestimmtes
chair	Stuhl
challenge	Herausforderung

change	Wechselgeld; Veränderung; Änderung; Wechsel
to **change**	umsteigen; wechseln; (sich) ändern; (sich) verändern
changing	im Wandel; wechselnd; sich verändernd
channel	Kanal; Programm; Sender
chapter	Kapitel
character	Figur; Charakter
to **charge**	aufladen; laden
charity	Wohltätigkeits-organisation
chart	Diagramm; Tabelle
to **chase**	jagen; verfolgen
chaser	Jäger/Jägerin; Verfolger/Verfolgerin
chat	Chat; Unterhaltung
to **chat**	chatten; plaudern
cheap	billig
to **check**	überprüfen; kontrollieren
check in	Einchecken
check out	Auschecken
cheeky	frech
cheerleader	Cheerleader/ Cheerleaderin
cheese	Käse
chef	Koch/Köchin
chemistry	Chemie
cherry	Kirsche
chicken	Hähnchen; Huhn
child, children	Kind, Kinder
chin	Kinn
China	China
Chinese	Chinesisch; chinesisch; aus China; Chinese/Chinesin
chips	Pommes frites
chocolate	Schokolade
to **choose**	auswählen; wählen
chore	Aufgabe; Arbeit
chorus	Refrain
chose	wählte (aus)
chosen	gewählt; ausgewählt
Christmas	Weihnachten
church	Kirche
cinema	Kino
city	Stadt; Großstadt
city break	Städtereise
civil rights	Bürgerrechte
to **clap**	klatschen
class	Klasse; Unterricht; Unterrichtsstunde
classmate	Mitschüler/Mitschülerin
classroom	Klassenzimmer
clean	sauber
to **clean (up)**	sauber machen; putzen
clever	schlau; klug
cliff	Klippe; Kliff
climate	Klima
to **climb**	steigen; klettern
climbing	Klettern
climbing wall	Kletterwand
clock	Uhr
clock tower	Uhrenturm
clog	Holzschuh; Clog
close	nah
to **close**	schließen; zumachen
closed	geschlossen; gesperrt
clothes	Kleider; Kleidung
cloud	Wolke
cloudy	wolkig
club	Klub; Schul-AG; Verein
coach	Trainer/Trainerin
coast	Küste
coat	Mantel; Jacke
coffin	Sarg
cola	Cola
cold	kalt; Erkältung; Schnupfen; Kälte
to **collapse**	einstürzen; zusammenbrechen
to **collect**	einsammeln; sammeln
college	College; Hochschule; Fachhochschule
colony	Kolonie
colour	Farbe
colourful	bunt; farbig
(to) **come, come**	kommen, gekommen
to **come in**	hereinkommen
comic	Comic; Comicheft
comment	Kommentar

communication	Kommunikation
community	Gemeinde; Gemeinschaft
company	Firma; Unternehmen; Gesellschaft
compass	Kompass
to **compete (in)**	antreten (bei); teilnehmen (an); sich messen
competition	Wettbewerb; Wettkampf; Turnier
to **complain**	sich beschweren; sich beklagen
computer	Computer
computer science	Informatik
concert	Konzert
confident	selbstsicher; selbstbewusst
confused	verwirrt; wirr
to **connect**	(sich) verbinden
connection	Verbindung; Zusammenhang
console	Konsole
to **contact**	sich in Verbindung setzen mit; kontaktieren
to **cook**	kochen
cooker	Herd
cookie	Keks
cool	cool; kühl
to **cope (with)**	bewältigen; fertig werden (mit)
corn	Mais; Korn
cornbread	Maisbrot
corner	Ecke
cost	Kosten; Preis
to **cost**	kosten
costume	Kostüm
cotton	Baumwolle
could	konnte
counseling *(AE)*	Beratung; psychologische Betreuung
to **count**	zählen
country	Land; ländliche Gegend
countryside	Land; Landschaft
court	Spielfeld
cousin	Cousin/Cousine
cow	Kuh
cowboy	Cowboy

craft	Handwerk
crazy	verrückt
cream	Sahne; Rahm; Creme
cream cheese	Frischkäse
to **create**	machen; schaffen; erschaffen
creative	kreativ
credit card	Kreditkarte
Cree	Cree-; Cree
creek *(AE)*	Bach
crew	Crew; Besatzung
criminal	Verbrecher/Verbrecherin
crisp	Kartoffelchip
to **cross**	überqueren
crowd	Menschenmenge
to **cry**	schreien; weinen; rufen
cucumber	Gurke
culture	Kultur
cup	Tasse
cupboard	Schrank
currency	Währung
curry	Curry
customer	Kunde/Kundin
(to) **cut, cut, cut**	(sich) schneiden, schnitt (sich), (sich) geschnitten
to **cycle**	Fahrrad fahren
cycle lane	Radweg
cycling	Radfahren

D

dad	Papa
daily	täglich; Alltags-
dairy	Milch-; Molkerei
to **damage**	beschädigen; schaden
dance	Tanz; Tanz-
to **dance**	tanzen
dancer	Tänzer/Tänzerin
dangerous	gefährlich
dark	dunkel
date	Datum; Termin; Verabredung; Date
daughter	Tochter
day	Tag
dead	tot; leer
Dear ...,	Liebe/Lieber ... *(Anrede in Briefen, E-Mails ...)*

death	Tod; Todesfall
December	Dezember
to **decide**	(sich) entscheiden
decoration	Dekoration; Schmuck
to **define**	definieren
definitely	auf jeden Fall; definitiv; eindeutig
degree	Grad; Hochschulabschluss; akademischer Grad;
degree Celsius (°C)	Grad Celsius
delayed	verspätet
to **deliver**	liefern
Denmark	Dänemark
departure hall	Abflughalle
to **describe**	beschreiben
description	Beschreibung
desert	Wüste
to **design**	entwerfen; gestalten; entwickeln
designer	Designer/Designerin; Entwickler/Entwicklerin
desk	Schreibtisch; Schalter
dessert	Nachspeise
to **destroy**	zerstören
to **detect**	entdecken; ermitteln
detention	Nachsitzen
device	Gerät; Vorrichtung
to **dial**	wählen *(Nummer)*
diary	Tagebuch
did	machte; tat
to **die**	sterben
different	unterschiedlich; anders
difficult	schwierig
to **dig**	graben
digital	digital
diner	amerikanisches Schnellrestaurant
dining room	Esszimmer
dinner	Abendessen
dinosaur	Dinosaurier
to **direct**	Regie führen (bei); anweisen; leiten
direction	Richtung
dirty	dreckig; schmutzig
disability	Behinderung
disaster	Katastrophe; Unglück
discipline	Disziplin
to **discriminate (against)**	diskriminieren; benachteiligen
discrimination	Diskriminierung
disease	Krankheit; Erkrankung
dish	Gericht; Geschirr
dishwasher	Spülmaschine
to **dispose (of)**	entsorgen
divided	geteilt; getrennt
to **do**	machen; tun
to **do babysitting**	babysitten
to **do handicrafts**	basteln
to **do sport**	Sport treiben
doctor	Arzt/Ärztin
dog	Hund
dog tag	Hundemarke
dollar ($)	Dollar *(amer. Währung)*
to **donate**	spenden
done	gemacht; getan
door	Tür
double-decker bus	Doppeldeckerbus
down	herunter; hinunter; entlang; (nach) unten
to **download**	herunterladen
dragon	Drache
drama	Theater; Drama
drank	trank
dream	Traum
dress	Kleid
dress code	Kleiderordnung
drink	Getränk
to **drink**	trinken
to **drive**	fahren; treiben
driven	gefahren; getrieben
driver	Fahrer/Fahrerin
drone	Drohne
to **drop**	fallen (lassen)
drove	fuhr; trieb
drug	Droge
drum	Trommel
drunk	getrunken; betrunken
dry	trocken
due to	wegen
dug, dug	grub, gegraben

dungeon	Verlies; Kerker
during	während
dye	Farbstoff
to **dye**	färben

E

each	jede/jeder/jedes
each other	einander; sich; sich gegenseitig
ear	Ohr
early	früh
earth	Erde; Boden
east	Osten; östlich
easy	einfach; leicht
to **eat**	essen
eaten	gegessen
e-book	E-Book
economy	Wirtschaft
editor	Redakteur/Redakteurin; Herausgeber/Herausgeberin
to **educate**	aufklären; bilden
education	Ausbildung; Bildung
egg	Ei
electrician	Elektriker/Elektrikerin
electricity	Strom; Elektrizität
elementary school *(AE)*	Grundschule
elevator *(AE)*	Aufzug; Lift
else	andere; sonst
email	E-Mail
emergency	Rettungs-; Not-; Notfall
emergency call	Notruf
emergency medical technician (EMT)	Rettungssanitäter/Rettungssanitäterin
emergency service	Notdienst; Rettungsdienst
emergency worker	Rettungskraft
empty	leer
to **encourage**	ermutigen; unterstützen
encyclopedia	Enzyklopädie; Lexikon
(to) **end**	aufhören; enden; beenden; Ende; Schluss
energy	Energie; Kraft
engineer	Ingenieur/Ingenieurin; Techniker/Technikerin
engineering	Maschinenbau; Technik
England	England
English	Englisch; englisch; aus England
English-speaking	englischsprachig; Englisch sprechend
to **enjoy**	genießen; mögen
enough	genug; genügend
entertainment	Unterhaltung
entrance	Eingang; Eintritt
entry	Eintrag
environment	Umwelt; Umgebung
equipment	Ausrüstung; Ausstattung
especially	insbesondere; besonders
euro	Euro *(Währung)*
Europe	Europa
European Union	Europäische Union
even	sogar; noch
evening	Abend
event	Ereignis; Veranstaltung
ever	jemals
every	jede/jeder/jedes
everybody	alle (zusammen); jeder
everyone	alle; jeder
everything	alles
everywhere	überall
exam	Prüfung
example	Beispiel
except	außer
exchange	Tausch; Austausch
to **exchange**	tauschen; austauschen; umtauschen
excited	aufgeregt
exciting	aufregend; spannend
Excuse me!	Entschuldigung!
exercise book	Übungsheft
exhausted	erschöpft
exhibition	Ausstellung
exit	Ausgang; Abgang; Ausfahrt
expensive	teuer
experience	Erfahrung; Erlebnis
experiment	Experiment
to **explain**	erklären; erläutern
to **extinguish**	ausmachen; löschen
extra	zusätzlich

extreme	extrem; radikal
eye	Auge

F

fabric	Stoff
face-to-face	persönlich
facility	Einrichtung
fact	Fakt; Tatsache
factory	Fabrik; Werk
fair	Messe; Jahrmarkt
fair	gerecht; fair
fairground	Rummelplatz
fairy	Fee
to **fall**	fallen
to **fall off**	herunterfallen; fallen
fallen	gefallen
family	Familie
famine	Hungersnot
famous	berühmt
fan	Fan
fancy dancer	Person, die einen traditionellen Tanz der amerikanischen Urbevölkerung vorführt
fantastic	fantastisch; großartig
far	weit; fern
farm	Bauernhof
farmer	Bauer/Bäuerin
farming	Landwirtschaft; Ackerbau
fascinating	faszinierend
fashion	Mode
fast	schnell
father	Vater
favorite *(AE)*, favourite *(BE)*	Lieblings-
feather	Feder
February	Februar
fee	Beitrag; Gebühr
to **feed**	füttern
to **feel**	(sich) fühlen; sich anfühlen
fell	fiel
felt, felt	fühlte (sich), (sich) gefühlt
fence	Zaun
ferry	Fähre
festival	Festival; Fest
fever	Fieber
field	Feld; Wiese; Weide
to **fight**	kämpfen; (sich) streiten
figure	Figur; Gestalt; Persönlichkeit
to **fill in**	ausfüllen
film	Film
final	letzte/letzter/letztes
finally	schließlich; endlich; zum Schluss
to **find (out)**	(heraus)finden,
fine	schön; fein
finger	Finger
to **finish**	enden; beenden; aufhören
fire	Feuer
fireworks	Feuerwerk
first	erste/erster/erstes
first aid	Erste Hilfe
firstly	erstens; zuerst
fish, fish	Fisch, Fische
fishing	Angeln; Fischen
fit	fit; in Form
to **fit**	passen
flag	Flagge; Fahne
flat	Wohnung
flat	flach; platt
flatbread	Fladenbrot
flew	flog
flight	Flug
flood	Überschwemmung; Flut; Hochwasser
floor	Fußboden; Stockwerk
flour	Mehl
flower	Blume
flown	geflogen
to **fly**	fliegen
fog	Nebel
to **fold**	falten; klappen; verschränken
folder	Ordner; Mappe
to **follow**	folgen; befolgen
food	Essen; Nahrung; Lebensmittel
foot	Fuß
football	Fußball
for	für

for example	zum Beispiel
for free	umsonst; kostenlos
foreign	ausländisch; fremd
forest	Wald
forever	für immer
to **forget**	vergessen
forgot	vergaß
forgotten	vergessen
form	Form; Formular
forward	nach vorne; vorwärts
fought, fought	kämpfte, gekämpft; stritten (sich), gestritten
to **found**	gründen
found, found	fand, gefunden
fountain	Springbrunnen
France	Frankreich
free	kostenlos; frei
to **free**	befreien
free time	Freizeit
free-time	Freizeit-
French	Französisch; französisch; aus Frankreich
fresh	frisch
Friday	Freitag
fridge	Kühlschrank
friend	Freund/Freundin
friendly	freundlich; nett
frog	Frosch
from	von; aus
front	Vorder-
fruit	Frucht; Obst
fun	Spaß; Freude; lustig
funeral	Beerdigung
funny	lustig; komisch; seltsam
future	Zukunft

G

gallery	Galerie
game	Spiel
to **game**	gamen; zocken
garden	Garten
gas	Gas
gave	gab; hielt *(Vortrag)*
geography	Erdkunde; Geografie
germ	Keim
German	Deutsch; deutsch; aus Deutschland
Germany	Deutschland
to **get**	werden; bekommen
to **get around**	herumkommen
to **get dressed**	sich anziehen
to **get hurt**	verletzt werden
to **get off**	aussteigen; absteigen; von Bord gehen
to **get out**	herauskommen; herausholen
to **get up**	aufstehen
to **get used (to sth)**	sich (an etw.) gewöhnen
ghost town	Geisterstadt
giant	riesig; Riesen-
giraffe	Giraffe
girl	Mädchen
girlfriend	Freundin
to **give**	geben; halten *(Vortrag)*
to **give away**	verschenken
to **give up**	aufgeben
given	gegeben; gehalten *(Vortrag)*
glass	Glas
glasses	Brille
global	weltweit; global
glove	Handschuh
to **go**	gehen; fahren
to **go cycling**	Fahrrad fahren
to **go dancing**	tanzen gehen
to **go hiking**	wandern gehen
to **go hunting**	auf die Jagd gehen; jagen gehen
to **go mad**	verrückt werden; ausrasten
to **go shopping**	einkaufen gehen
to **go sightseeing**	eine Besichtigungstour machen
to **go swimming**	schwimmen gehen
to **go walking**	spazieren gehen; wandern gehen
goal	Tor; Ziel
goat	Ziege
gold	Gold
gold rush	Goldrausch
gold-mining	Goldabbau
good	gut
Good luck!	Viel Glück!
Good morning.	Guten Morgen.

Goodbye.	Auf Wiedersehen.
gorilla	Gorilla
gospel	Gospel *(Musikrichtung)*
got, got	wurde, geworden; bekam, bekommen
graffiti	Graffiti
grandma	Oma
grandpa	Opa
grandparents	Großeltern
grass	Gras; Rasen
grave	Grab
great	toll; großartig; groß
Great Britain	Großbritannien
grew	wuchs; baute an; züchtete
grizzly bear	Grizzlybär
ground	Boden; Erdboden
ground floor	Erdgeschoss
ground level	Erdgeschoss
grounds	Anlage; Gelände
group	Gruppe
to **grow**	wachsen; anbauen; züchten
to **grow up**	aufwachsen
grown	gewachsen; angebaut; gezüchtet
guest	Gast
guide	Führer/Führerin
guitar	Gitarre
guy	Typ; Kerl
guys	Leute
gym	Turnhalle; Fitnessstudio

H

had	hatte
hairbrush	Haarbürste
hairdresser's	Friseursalon
hairdryer	Föhn
ham	Schinken
hammer	Hammer
hammer throw	Hammerwerfen
hand	Hand
to **hand over**	abgeben; übergeben
handicraft	Handarbeit
handout	Handout
to **hang out (with)**	rumhängen (mit); sich treffen (mit)
to **hang up**	auflegen; aufhängen
to **happen**	geschehen; passieren
happy	glücklich
hard	hart; schwierig
hardly	kaum
has	hat
hat	Hut
to **hate**	hassen
to **have a shower**	duschen
to **have got**	haben
to **have to**	müssen
had, had	hatte, gehabt
he	er
head	Kopf
headache	Kopfschmerzen
health	Gesundheit
healthy	gesund
to **hear**	hören
heard, heard	hörte, gehört
heart	Herz
heavy	schwer; stark
heavy cream	Sahne mit sehr hohem Fettgehalt
Hello there.	Hallo.; Grüß dich.
Hello.	Hallo.
(to) **help**	Hilfe; helfen
helpless	hilflos; machtlos
her	ihr/ihre; sie
here	hier
Here you are.	Bitte schön.
hero	Held/Heldin
Hi.	Hi.; Hallo.
high	hoch; groß
high school	Highschool
high street	Hauptstraße
highlight	Highlight; Höhepunkt
to **hijack**	entführen; kapern
to **hike**	wandern
hiking	Wandern
hill	Hügel; Berg
him	ihm; ihn
his	sein/seine
Hispanic	lateinamerikanisch; aus Lateinamerika; Lateinamerikaner/Lateinamerikanerin

history	Geschichte
(to) **hit, hit, hit**	treffen, traf, getroffen; schlagen, schlug, geschlagen
to **hold**	(fest)halten; tragen
held, held	hielt (fest), (fest) gehalten
hole	Loch
holiday	Ferien; Urlaub; Feiertag
holiday cottage	Ferienhäuschen
holiday flat	Ferienwohnung
home	Zuhause; Heim
homeless	obdachlos; Obdachlosen-
homeroom *(AE)*	Treffpunkt vor der ersten Stunde, u. a. zur Überprüfung der Anwesenheit
homework	Hausaufgabe, Hausaufgaben
honest	ehrlich
hope	Hoffnung
to **hope**	hoffen
horse	Pferd
horse riding	Reiten
hospital	Krankenhaus
host	Gastgeber/Gastgeberin
hot	heiß
hot dog	Hotdog
hotel	Hotel
hour	Stunde
house	Haus
houseboat	Hausboot
how	wie
How are you?	Wie geht es dir?
How much (is/are) ...?	Wie viel (kostet/kosten) ...?
How old are you?	Wie alt bist du?
How to ...	Wie man ...
however	jedoch
to **hug**	umarmen
human	Mensch; menschlich
hung up	legte auf, aufgelegt; hängte auf, aufgehängt
hungry	hungrig
(to) **hunt**	Jagd; jagen
hunter	Jäger/Jägerin
hurricane	Orkan; Wirbelsturm; Hurrikan
(to) **hurt, hurt, hurt**	weh tun, tat weh, weh getan; verletzen, verletzte, verletzt
husband	Ehemann

I

I	ich
I can't wait.	Ich kann es kaum erwarten.
I don't like ...	Ich mag ... nicht; ... gefällt mir nicht.
I wish you were here.	Ich wünschte, du wärst hier.
I'd like ... (= I would like)	Ich hätte gerne ...; Ich würde gerne ...
I'm from ...	Ich komme aus ...
I'm sorry.	Es tut mir leid.
ice cream	Eiscreme; Eis
ice hockey	Eishockey
ice pack	Eisbeutel; Kühlakku
ice skating	Schlittschuhlaufen
idea	Idee; Ahnung
if	wenn; falls; ob
to **ignore**	ignorieren
iguana	Leguan
ill	krank; schlecht
immediately	sofort
immigrant	Einwanderer/ Einwanderin
to **immigrate**	einwandern
important	wichtig; einflussreich
to **improve**	verbessern
in	in
in front of	vor; davor
in my opinion	meiner Meinung nach
in the country	auf dem Land
in the evening(s)	abends
in the world	(in) der Welt
to **include**	beinhalten; einschließen
India	Indien
Indian	Indisch; indisch; aus Indien; Inder/Inderin
industry	Industrie
to **influence**	beeinflussen
influencer	Influencer/Influencerin

info (= information)	Info (= Information)
to **inform**	informieren
information	Information
information desk	Information; Auskunft
injury	Verletzung
inside	in; innen in; im Innern
to **inspire**	inspirieren
to **install**	installieren; einrichten; anschließen
instrument	Instrument
to **insult**	beleidigen
interest	Interesse
interesting	interessant
international	international
internet	Internet
internship	Praktikum
to **interrupt**	unterbrechen
interview	Interview; Befragung
into	in; hinein
introduction	Einleitung; Einführung
invitation	Einladung
to **invite**	bitten; auffordern; einladen
Irish	Irisch; irisch; aus Irland
is	ist
island	Insel
it	es
IT	Informatik
Italian	Italienisch; italienisch; aus Italien; Italiener/Italienerin
Italy	Italien
its	ihr/ihre; sein/seine

J

jam	Marmelade; Konfitüre
January	Januar
jazz	Jazz
jeans	Jeans
jewellery	Schmuck
Jewish	jüdisch
job	Job; Arbeit; Beruf; Aufgabe
to **join**	sich anschließen; beitreten; Mitglied werden in
joke	Witz; Scherz
journey	Fahrt; Reise
juice	Saft
July	Juli
to **jump**	springen
to **jump in**	reinspringen
June	Juni
junk	Gerümpel; Schrott
junk food	Junkfood; ungesundes Essen
just	gerade eben; nur; einfach

K

kangaroo	Känguru
kayaking	Kajakfahren
kebab	Döner
to **keep in touch**	in Verbindung bleiben
to **keep up (with)**	mithalten (mit)
to **keep up to date**	auf dem neuesten Stand bleiben
kept, kept	behielt, behalten; hielt, gehalten; bewahrte auf, aufbewahrt
keyword	Stichwort; Schlüsselbegriff
kid	Kind
to **kill**	töten
kilogramme (kg)	Kilogramm
kilometre (km)	Kilometer
kilt	Schottenrock; Kilt
kind	Art; Sorte
king	König
to **kiss**	küssen
kitchen	Küche
knee	Knie
knee catch	Fußballtrick *(bei dem der Ball mit den Knien aufgefangen und eingeklemmt wird)*
knew	wusste; kannte
to **know**	wissen; kennen
known	gewusst; gekannt; bekannt

L

lacrosse	Lacrosse *(Ballsportart)*
lake	See

lamp	Lampe
to **land**	landen
landscape	Landschaft
language	Sprache
large	groß
last	letzte/letzter/letztes
to **last**	dauern; andauern; anhalten
late	spät; zu spät
later	später
to **laugh**	lachen
launch site	Raketenabschussbasis
laverbread	Algenpaste
law	Gesetz
to **lead**	anführen; führen; leiten; anleiten
leader	Leiter/Leiterin; Anführer/Anführerin
leaflet	Broschüre; Informationsblatt; Prospekt
to **learn**	erfahren; lernen
led, led	führte (an), angeführt; leitete (an), (an)geleitet
to **learn about sth**	etwas über etw. erfahren
learning	Lernen
to **leave**	abfahren; verlassen; lassen
left, left	verließ, verlassen; fuhr ab, abgefahren; ließ, gelassen
left	links
leg	Bein
legend	Legende; Sage
lemon	Zitrone
lemonade	Limonade
less	weniger
lesson	Schulstunde
let's (= let us)	lass(t) uns
letter	Brief; Buchstabe
library	Bibliothek; Bücherei
license *(AE)*	Lizenz; Erlaubnis
life	Leben
life cycle	Lebenszyklus; Lebensdauer; Laufzeit
lift	Aufzug; Fahrstuhl; Lift
to **lift**	heben; hochheben; anheben

light	Licht
to **light**	anzünden; erhellen
lighthouse	Leuchtturm
lighting	Beleuchtung
like	wie
to **like**	mögen
line	Verbindung; Linie; Zeile
lion	Löwe
to **listen (to)**	zuhören; anhören; hören
listener	Zuhörer/Zuhörerin
lit, lit	zündete an, angezündet; erhellte, erhellt
litter	Müll; Abfall
little	klein
little person	Kleinwüchsiger/ Kleinwüchsige
to **live**	wohnen; leben
living	Leben; Wohnen
living room	Wohnzimmer
to **load**	einräumen; (be)laden
local	lokal; örtlich
locals	Einheimische; Ortsansässige
loch	See *(in Schottland)*
locker	Schließfach; Spind
log	Holzstamm
to **log in**	einloggen
long	lang; lange
to **look**	sehen; aussehen
to **look after**	aufpassen auf; hüten; sich kümmern um
to **look at**	anschauen
to **look for**	suchen nach
to **look forward (+ -ing)**	sich freuen auf
to **lose**	verlieren
lost, lost	verlor, verloren; verschwunden
lost and found	Fundbüro; Fundsachen
lots (of)	viel; jede Menge
loud	laut
to **love**	lieben
low	niedrig
luck	Glück
luggage	Gepäck
lunch	Mittagessen

lunchbox	Brotdose
lunchtime	Mittagszeit

M

machine	Maschine; Gerät
made, made	machte, gemacht; tat, getan; stellte her, hergestellt
magazine	Zeitschrift
magic	magisch; Zauberkraft; Magie; Zauberei
to **make**	machen; tun; herstellen
to **make a mess**	Unordnung/Dreck machen
to **make friends**	Freundschaften schließen
to **make sure**	dafür sorgen; sich versichern
man, men	Mann, Männer
mango	Mango
many	viele
map	Landkarte; Stadtplan
March	März
to **march**	marschieren
marching band	Blaskapelle; Marschkapelle
market	Markt
Mars	Mars
mashed potatoes	Kartoffelbrei
match	Spiel
material	Material; Stoff
math *(AE)*, **maths** *(BE)*	Mathematik; Mathe
May	Mai
may	dürfen; können
Mayan	Maya
maybe	vielleicht
mayor	Bürgermeister/ Bürgermeisterin
me	mich; mir
meal	Essen; Mahlzeit
to **mean**	meinen; bedeuten
means of transport	Transportmittel; Verkehrsmittel
meat	Fleisch
media	Medien; Medien-
medicine	Medizin; Medikamente
to **meet**	treffen; kennenlernen,
meeting	Treffen; Besprechung
member	Mitglied
membership	Mitgliedschaft
memorial	Denkmal; Gedenkstätte
mess	Unordnung; Durcheinander
message	Nachricht; SMS
met, met	traf, getroffen; lernte kennen, kennengelernt
metal	Metall
metal detector	Metalldetektor
meter (m) *(AE)*, **metre** *(BE)*	Meter
microwave	Mikrowelle
middle	Mitte
mile	Meile
military	militärisch
milk	Milch
to **milk**	melken
million	Million
mine	meine/meiner/meins
to **mine**	abbauen; graben nach
minute	Minute
to **miss**	vermissen; verpassen
mission	Mission; Auftrag
mistake	Fehler
mix	Mischung
mixed	gemischt
model	Model; Modell; Vorlage
modern	modern
mom *(AE)*, **mum** *(BE)*	Mama
moment	Moment; Augenblick
monarch	Monarch/Monarchin
Monday	Montag
money	Geld
monster	Monster; Ungeheuer
month	Monat
moon	Mond
more	mehr; weitere
morning	Morgen; Vormittag
(the) most	am meisten; die meisten; die Mehrheit
mostly	größtenteils; meistens; hauptsächlich

mother	Mutter
mountain	Berg
mouse	Maus
mouth	Mund; Maul
to **move**	versetzen; bewegen; umziehen
movement	Bewegung
movie *(AE)*	Film
Mr	Herr *(Anrede)*
Mrs	Frau *(Anrede)*
Ms	Frau *(Anrede)*
much	viel
multicultural	multikulturell
multimedia	Multimedia-; multimedial
mural	Wandbild; Wandgemälde
museum	Museum
music	Musik
musician	Musiker/Musikerin
must	müssen
mustn't	nicht dürfen
my	mein/meine
mystery	Rätsel; Geheimnis

N

(to) **name**	Name; benennen
narrator	Erzähler/Erzählerin
national	national
national park	Nationalpark; Naturpark
Native American	amerikanischer Ureinwohner / amerikanische Ureinwohnerin
natural	Natur-; natürlich
nature	Natur
Navajo	Navajo; Navajo-
near	in der Nähe von
neck	Hals; Nacken; Genick
to **need**	brauchen
needle	Nadel
needn't	nicht müssen; nicht brauchen
negative	negativ; ablehnend
negative about	ablehnend gegenüber
neighbour	Nachbar/Nachbarin
neighbourhood	Viertel; Nachbarschaft
nervous	nervös
never	nie; niemals
new	neu
New Year	Neujahr
news	Nachrichten; Neuigkeiten
newspaper	Zeitung
next	nächste/nächster/nächstes
next to	neben
nice	schön; nett
Nice to meet you.	Schön, dich kennenzulernen.
Nigeria	Nigeria
night	Nacht; Abend
no	nein; kein/keine
no one	niemand
nobody	niemand
to **nod**	nicken
noise	Geräusch; Lärm
noisy	laut
non-	nicht-
Norman	Normanne/Normannin; normannisch
north	Norden; nördlich
Northern Ireland	Nordirland
nose	Nase
nosy	neugierig
not	nicht
not anyone	niemand
not ... either	auch nicht
not ... anymore *(AE)*	nicht mehr
not ... yet	noch nicht
November	November
now	jetzt; nun
number	Zahl; Nummer; Anzahl
nurse	Pflegefachmann/Pflegefachfrau
nut	Nuss

O

o'clock	Uhr *(Zeitangabe bei vollen Stunden)*
ocean	Ozean; Meer
October	Oktober
of	von
of course	natürlich; selbstverständlich

to **offer**	anbieten; bieten
office	Büro
official	offiziell
official language	Amtssprache
often	oft; häufig
oh well	was soll's
oil	Öl
OK	okay
old	alt
on	an; auf; über
on foot	zu Fuß
on the left	auf der linken Seite; links
on time	pünktlich
once	einmal
one another	einander; gegenseitig
one(s)	Platzhalter für ein Nomen
onion	Zwiebel
online	online
only	nur
only child	Einzelkind
open	geöffnet; offen
to **open**	öffnen; aufmachen
opening times	Öffnungszeiten
operator	Vermittlung; Telefonist/Telefonistin
opposite	gegenüber
or	oder
orange	Orange
orang-utan	Orang-Utan
order	Bestell-; Bestellung
to **order**	bestellen
organic	Bio-; organisch
organisation	Organisation
to **organize** *(AE)*	organisieren; ordnen
other	andere; weitere
others	andere
our	unser/unsere
out and about	unterwegs
out of ...	aus ... heraus; von ...
outdoor	Outdoor-; Freiluft-
outreach	Hilfe
outreach center *(AE)*	Beratungsstelle
outside	(nach) draußen; vor
over	über; vorbei
over there	da drüben; dort drüben
own	eigene/eigener/eigenes
owner	Besitzer/Besitzerin

P

p.m.	nachmittags *(Uhrzeit)*
package	Paket; verpacken
packet	Packung; Tüte
page	Seite; Blatt
paid, paid	bezahlte, bezahlt
pain	Schmerz
to **paint**	(an)malen; streichen
pair of	Paar
palace	Palast
pancake	Pfannkuchen; Eierkuchen
panic	Panik
paper	Papier
parade	Parade; Umzug
paradise	Paradies
paralympic	paralympisch
paramedic	Sanitäter/Sanitäterin
pardon	Entschuldigung
parents	Eltern
park	Park
part	Gegend; Teil
partner	Partner/Partnerin
party	Party; Feier
passenger	Fluggast; Passagier/Passagierin
passport	Pass; Reisepass
past	Vergangenheit; vorbei (an)
pasta	Nudeln; Pasta
path	Weg; Pfad
patient	Patient/Patientin
patient	geduldig
to **pay**	bezahlen
PE (= Physical Education)	Sportunterricht
pea	Erbse
peace	Frieden
peaceful	friedlich
pecan	Pekannuss
pen	Füller; Stift

pencil case	Federmäppchen
people	Leute; Menschen
pepper	Paprika; Pfeffer
per	pro
percent (%)	Prozent (%)
perfect	perfekt; vollkommen
person	Person
person of color (POC) ***(AE)***	Person mit dunkler Hautfarbe
pet	Haustier
phone	Handy; Telefon
phone call	Telefonanruf
photo	Foto
photographer	Fotograf/Fotografin
to **pick up**	aufheben
picnic	Picknick
picture	Bild
pie	Kuchen; Pastete
pier	Pier; Hafendamm
pig	Schwein
pitch	Spielfeld; Platz
pizza	Pizza
place	Ort; Platz; Stelle
plain	einfach; schlicht
plan	Plan
to **plan**	planen
plane	Flugzeug
planet	Planet
plant	Pflanze
to **plant**	pflanzen
plantain	Kochbanane
plaster	Pflaster
plastic	Plastik; Kunststoff
plate	Teller
platform	Bahnsteig; Plattform
play	Theaterstück
to **play**	spielen
player	Spieler/Spielerin
playground	Schulhof; Spielplatz
please	bitte
Pledge of Allegiance	Treueeid
pocket	Tasche; Hosentasche
podcast	Podcast
point	Punkt; Komma *(bei Dezimalzahlen)*; Zeitpunkt; Sinn
poison	Gift
police	Polizei
police officer	Polizeibeamter/ Polizeibeamtin
Polish	Polnisch; polnisch; aus Polen
polite	höflich
pond	Teich
pool	Schwimmbecken; Teich
popular	beliebt
population	Einwohnerzahl; Einwohner *(Pl.)*; Bevölkerung
Portugal	Portugal
positive	positiv
possible	möglich
post	Beitrag; Post
to **post**	posten; online stellen
post box	Briefkasten
pot	Topf
potato	Kartoffel
potion	Trank
pound	Pfund *(brit. Währungseinheit)*
power	Energie; Strom; Kraft; Macht
powerful	stark; mächtig; beeindruckend
powwow	Versammlung *(der ursprünglichen Völker Nordamerikas)*
practical	praktisch
to **practise**	üben; trainieren
to **prepare**	(sich) vorbereiten
present	Geschenk
to **present**	präsentieren; vorstellen
presentation	Präsentation; Vortrag
president	Präsident/Präsidentin
to **press**	drücken; pressen
prime minister	Premierminister/ Premierministerin; Ministerpräsident/ Ministerpräsidentin
prince	Prinz
print	gedruckt
printer	Drucker
probably	wahrscheinlich
problem	Problem

to **process**	verarbeiten; aufbereiten; verstehen
to **produce**	herstellen; produzieren; erzeugen; anbauen
product	Produkt
production	Produktion; Herstellung
to **program**	programmieren
program *(BE)*	Computerprogramm
programmer	Programmierer/ Programmiererin
project	Projekt
to **promote**	bewerben
to **protect**	schützen; beschützen
(to) **protest**	Protest; Demonstration; protestieren
Protestant	Protestant/ Protestantin; protestantisch
protesting	protestierend
proud (of)	stolz (auf)
pub	Kneipe; Gasthaus
public	öffentlich
to **pull**	ziehen
pumpkin	Kürbis
punch	Punsch; Bowle
purple	lila; violett
to **push**	schubsen; drängeln; schieben; drücken
to **put on**	anziehen; anlegen; draufmachen
to **put sth in a bin**	etw. in einen Mülleimer werfen
to **put together**	zusammensetzen; zusammenbauen
to **put up**	aufhängen; aufstellen; hochhalten; errichten
(to) **put, put, put**	legen, legte, gelegt; bringen, brachte, gebracht; setzen, setzte, gesetzt; stellen, stellte, gestellt
puzzle	Rätsel; Puzzle

Q

quality	Qualität; Eigenschaft
queen	Königin
question	Frage
queue	Warteschlange
quick	schnell
quiet	leise; still; ruhig
quite	ziemlich

R

race	Wettrennen; Rennen
racism	Rassismus
radio	Radio
railway	Eisenbahn
rain	Regen
to **rain**	regnen
rainy	regnerisch
to **raise awareness**	das Bewusstsein schärfen; jdn. sensibilisieren
to **raise money**	Geld sammeln
ran	lief; rannte
rat	Ratte
raw material	Rohstoff; Rohmaterial
to **reach out**	die Hand ausstrecken
(to) **read, read, read**	lesen, las, gelesen
real	echt; richtig; wirklich
really	wirklich; echt; sehr
reason	Grund
to **rebuild**	wiederaufbauen
to **receive**	bekommen; erhalten
recipe	Rezept
record	Rekord
recording	Aufnahme
recording studio	Tonstudio
to **recycle**	recyceln; wiederverwerten
region	Region; Gegend
registration	Anwesenheitskontrolle
relative	Verwandter/Verwandte
to **relax**	sich entspannen; sich ausruhen
religious	religiös; gläubig
to **remember**	sich erinnern (an); sich merken
to **remove**	entfernen
to **renovate**	renovieren; sanieren
rent	Miete
to **rent**	mieten
to **repair**	reparieren
repair service	Reparaturdienst
to **repeat**	wiederholen

rescue	Rettung
rescuer	Retter/Retterin
research	Forschung; Recherche
reservation	Reservat
to **respect**	respektieren
to **respect each other**	einander respektieren
restaurant	Restaurant
to **return**	zurückschicken; zurückgeben; zurückkehren
rice	Reis
rich	reich
ride	Fahrt; Ritt
to **ride**	fahren; reiten
right	rechts; richtig; Recht
right now	gerade; jetzt gerade; sofort
ring	Ring
riot	Ausschreitung; Unruhe
river	Fluss
road	Straße
robin	Rotkehlchen
robot	Roboter; Roboter-
rock	Fels; Stein
rode	fuhr; ritt
rodeo	Rodeo
role	Rolle
role model	Vorbild
role play	Rollenspiel
roller coaster	Achterbahn
Roman	Römer/Römerin; römisch
roof	Dach
room	Zimmer; Raum; Platz
round	rund
routine	Routine; Ablauf
rugby	Rugby
rule	Regel
(to) **run, run**	laufen, gelaufen; rennen, gerannt
runner	Läufer/Läuferin
running	Laufen
Russia	Russland

S

sad	traurig
safe	in Sicherheit; sicher
said, said	sagte, gesagt; sprach, gesprochen
salad	Salat
salary	Gehalt
sale	Verkauf; Ausverkauf
salt	Salz
sandwich	Sandwich; belegtes Brot
sang	sang
sat, sat	saß, gesessen
Saturday	Samstag
sauce	Soße
sausage	Wurst; Bratwurst
to **save**	sparen; retten; speichern
saw	sah
to **say**	sagen; sprechen
Scandinavia	Skandinavien
scared	verängstigt
scarf	Schal; Tuch
scary	gruselig
scene	Szene; Schauplatz; Situation
school	Schule
science	Wissenschaft; Naturwissenschaft
scientist	Wissenschaftler/ Wissenschaftlerin
Scotland	Schottland
Scottish	Schottisch; schottisch; aus Schottland
scrapbook	Scrapbook *(selbst gestaltetes Buch)*; Sammelalbum
screensaver	Bildschirmschoner
script	Drehbuch; Skript
sea	Meer
seafood	Meeresfrüchte
seafront	Meeresufer
seaside	Küste; Küsten-
season	Jahreszeit; Saison
seat	Sitz; Sitzplatz
second	Sekunde
second-hand	gebraucht; secondhand
secondly	zweitens
secret	geheim
secretary	Schriftführer/ Schriftführerin
secure	sicher
security	Sicherheit

to **see**	sehen
See you later.	Tschüss.; Bis bald.
See you soon.	Bis bald.
seen	gesehen
seed	Samen; Saat
segregation	Rassentrennung
to **sell**	verkaufen
to **send**	schicken; senden
sent, sent	schickte, geschickt; sendete, gesendet
sentence	Satz
September	September
serious	ernsthaft; schwer
service	Dienst; Service
set	Set; Kulisse
to **settle (in)**	sich niederlassen (in); besiedeln
settler	Siedler/Siedlerin
to **sew**	nähen
sewed, sewn	nähte, genäht
shake	schütteln; zittern
shampoo	Shampoo
shamrock	Kleeblatt
to **share**	teilen
shark	Hai
she	sie
shelf, shelves	Regal, Regale; Regalbrett, Regalbretter
ship	Schiff
shirt	Shirt; Hemd
shocked	schockiert; geschockt
shoe	Schuh
shook	schüttelte; zitterte
to **shoot (at)**	schießen
shop	Laden; Geschäft
shopping	Einkaufen
shopping centre	Einkaufszentrum
short	kurz
shot put	Kugelstoßen
should	sollte
shoulder	Schulter
to **shout**	schreien; rufen
show	Show; Aufführung
to **show**	zeigen
to **show sb around (a place)**	jdn. (an einem Ort) herumführen
shower	Dusche
shower gel	Duschgel
(to) **shut, shut, shut**	zumachen, machte zu, zugemacht; schließen, schloss, geschlossen
shy	schüchtern
side	Seite
sidewalk *(AE)*	Gehweg; Bürgersteig
sight	Sehenswürdigkeit
sightseeing	Besichtigung; Sightseeing
sign	Schild; Zeichen
signal	Empfang; Signal
silly	blöd; dumm; albern
since	seit; seitdem
Sincerely,	Mit freundlichen Grüßen
to **sing**	singen
singer	Sänger/Sängerin
sink	Waschbecken; Spülbecken
sister	Schwester
to **sit**	sitzen
to **sit down**	sich hinsetzen; sich setzen
site	Gelände; Ort; Schauplatz
situation	Situation
size	Größe
skate park	Skatepark
skateboard	Skateboard
skill	Fähigkeit; Kenntnis
skin	Haut; Fell
skirt	Rock
sky	Himmel
skyscraper	Wolkenkratzer
slave	Sklave/Sklavin
slavery	Sklaverei
to **sleep**	schlafen
sleeve	Ärmel
slept, slept	schlief, geschlafen
slide	Folie
slide show	Bildschirmpräsentation
slow	langsam
small	klein
smart	schlau; intelligent; schick
to **smell**	riechen
smelled/smelt, smelled/smelt	roch, gerochen

smile	lächeln
smoking	Rauchen
snack	Snack; Imbiss
snack bar	Café; Imbissstube
snake	Schlange
(to) **snow**	Schnee; schneien
so	so; also; daher
so far	bisher; bislang; bis jetzt
soap	Seife
social	sozial; gesellschaftlich
social media	soziale Medien
social work	Sozialarbeit
sofa	Sofa
software	Software
solar	Sonnen-; Solar-; solar
solar panel	Sonnenkollektor; Solarpaneel
solar system	Sonnensystem
sold, sold	verkaufte, verkauft
solution	Lösung
to **solve**	lösen
solving puzzles	Rätselraten; Lösen von Rätseln
some	ein paar; einige; manche
someone	jemand
something	etwas
sometimes	manchmal
son	Sohn
soon	bald; schnell
Sorry.	Tut mir leid.; Entschuldigung.
sound	Ton; Laut; Geräusch
to **sound**	klingen; sich anhören
soup	Suppe
south	Süden; südlich
souvenir	Souvenir; Andenken
soy	Soja
space	Weltraum; Platz
space shuttle	Raumfähre
space station	Raumstation
space travel	Raumfahrt
spacecraft	Raumschiff
Spain	Spanien
Spanish	Spanisch; spanisch; aus Spanien
to **speak**	sprechen
speaker	Sprecher/Sprecherin; Redner/Rednerin
special	besonders; speziell
speech	Rede; Sprache
to **spell**	buchstabieren
to **spend**	verbringen; ausgeben *(Geld)*
spent, spent	verbrachte, verbracht; gab aus, ausgegeben *(Geld)*
spiky	stachlig
spooky	gespenstisch
sport	Sport; Sportart
sports event	Sportveranstaltung
spot	Fleck; Stelle; Ort
spotlight	Rampenlicht; Scheinwerfer
spring	Frühling; Frühjahr
square	Platz; Quadrat
square kilometre (km^2)	Quadratkilometer
square mile	Quadratmeile
squirrel	Eichhörnchen
stadium	Stadion
staff	Personal; Belegschaft
stairs	Treppe; Treppenhaus
to **stand**	stehen
to **stand up**	aufstehen; stehen
to **stand up to sb**	sich gegen jdn. behaupten
star	Stern
to **start**	anfangen; starten
start-up	Start-up
state	Bundesstaat; Staat; Land; Zustand
statement	Aussage; Behauptung; Erklärung
station	Station; Bahnhof
statue	Statue; Standbild
stay	Aufenthalt
to **stay**	bleiben; übernachten
to **steal**	stehlen
steel	Stahl
step	Schritt; Stufe
stew	Eintopf
sticker	Aufkleber
still	immer noch; noch; trotzdem

stole	stahl
stolen	gestohlen
stomach ache	Bauchschmerzen
stone	Stein
stood, stood	stand, gestanden
stop	Halt; Haltestelle
to **stop**	anhalten; stehen bleiben; aufhören
store ***(AE)***	Laden; Geschäft
storm	Sturm
story	Geschichte
story ***(AE)***	Etage; Stockwerk
straight	gerade; direkt
straight on	geradeaus
strange	merkwürdig; seltsam
strategy	Strategie; Vorgehensweise
to **stream**	streamen *(im Internet)*
street	Straße
street art	Straßenkunst
strength	Stärke; Kraft
stressful	anstrengend
strike	Streik
strong	stark
student	Schüler/Schülerin; Student/Studentin
student council	Schülerrat
studio	Studio; Atelier
to **study**	studieren; lernen
stupid	dumm; blöd
subject	Schulfach
submarine	U-Boot
subway ***(AE)***	U-Bahn
successful	erfolgreich
suddenly	plötzlich; auf einmal
sugar	Zucker
summer	Sommer
sun	Sonne
sun cream	Sonnencreme
Sunday	Sonntag
sunflower	Sonnenblume
sung	gesungen
sunglasses	Sonnenbrille
sunny	sonnig
suntan	Sonnenbräune
supermarket	Supermarkt
support	Hilfe; Unterstützung
to **support**	unterstützen
sure	sicher
surfing	Surfen
surprised	überrascht
survey	Umfrage
to **survive**	überleben
sustainable	zukunftsfähig; nachhaltig
swam	schwamm
sweater	Pullover
to **swim**	schwimmen
swimmer	Schwimmer/ Schwimmerin
swimming	Schwimmen
swimming pool	Schwimmbad
Switzerland	die Schweiz
sword	Schwert
swum	geschwommen
symbol	Symbol
Syrian	syrisch; aus Syrien; Syrer/Syrerin

T

table	Tisch
tablet	Tablet; Tablette
to **take**	(mit)nehmen; dauern
to **take a look at sth**	(sich) etw. ansehen
to **take a seat**	sich hinsetzen
to **take care of ...**	sich um ... kümmern; für ... sorgen
to **take out**	herausnehmen; herausbringen
to **take part (in)**	teilnehmen (an)
to **take photos**	Fotos machen
to **take place**	stattfinden
to **take sb/sth seriously**	jdn./etw. ernst nehmen
to **take the dog for a walk**	den Hund spazieren führen
taken	(mit)genommen; gedauert
talented	talentiert; begabt
to **talk (to)**	sprechen (mit); reden (mit)
tall	groß; hoch
task	Aufgabe; Auftrag

to **taste**	schmecken
tasty	lecker; schmackhaft
taught, taught	brachte bei, beigebracht; unterrichtete, unterrichtet
taxi	Taxi
tea	Tee; frühes Abendessen
to **teach**	beibringen; unterrichten
teacher	Lehrer/Lehrerin
team	Team; Mannschaft
to **tear down**	abreißen; zerstören; abbrechen
technical	technisch
technology	Technik; Technologie
teenager	Teenager; Jugendlicher/Jugendliche
to **tell**	sagen; erzählen
temperature	Temperatur
tennis	Tennis
tent	Zelt
terrible	schrecklich; schlimm; furchtbar
terrorist	Terrorist/Terroristin; Terror-
text	Text
than	als
Thank you.	Danke.
thanks	danke
Thanksgiving	Erntedankfest
that	dass; der/die/das
That's £4.40.	Das macht vier Pfund und 40 Pence.
the	der; die *(auch Pl.)*; das
the British Isles	die Britischen Inseln
the French	die Franzosen
the others	die anderen
the Republic of Ireland	Irland
the same ...	derselbe/dieselbe/dasselbe ...; der/die/das gleiche ...
the Troubles	Unruhen in Nordirland im 20. Jahrhundert
the UK (United Kingdom)	das Vereinigte Königreich
the USA (United States of America)	die USA (Vereinigte Staaten von Amerika)
theatre	Theater
their	ihr *(Pl.)*; ihre *(Pl.)*
them	sie *(Pl.)*; ihnen
then	danach; dann
there	da; dort
there are	da sind; es gibt
there is	da ist; es gibt
these	das; diese (hier)
they	sie *(Pl.)*
thigh	Oberschenkel
thing	Sache; Ding
to **think**	finden; denken; glauben
thirsty	durstig
this	das; dies
this morning	heute Morgen
those	diese dort; jene
thought	Gedanke
thought, thought	dachte, gedacht; glaubte, geglaubt
threw	warf
through	durch
to **throw**	werfen
to **throw away**	wegwerfen
thrown	geworfen
Thursday	Donnerstag
ticket	Fahrkarte; Eintrittskarte
ticket office	Fahrkartenschalter
time	Uhrzeit; Zeit; Mal
time zone	Zeitzone
tip	Tipp; Ratschlag
tired	müde
to	in; zu; nach; bis
toast	Toast
today	heute
tofu	Tofu
together	zusammen; gemeinsam
toilet	Toilette
told	sagte, gesagt; erzählte, erzählt
tomato	Tomate
tomorrow	morgen
tonight	heute Abend; heute Nacht
too	auch; zu
took	nahm (mit); dauerte

tool	Werkzeug; Gerät
tooth, teeth	Zahn, Zähne
toothbrush	Zahnbürste
top	beste/bester/bestes; Top-
top	Top; Oberteil
topic	Thema
tore down	riss ab; zerstörte; brach ab
torn down	abgerissen; zerstört; abgebrochen
tornado	Tornado; Wirbelsturm
to touch	anfassen; berühren
tour	Rundgang; Tour; Reise; Führung
tourist	Tourist/Touristin
tourist information centre	Touristeninformation
towel	Handtuch
tower	Turm
town	Stadt
town hall	Rathaus
town hall meeting	Bürgerversammlung
toy	Spielzeug
track	Strecke; Gleis
track and field	Leichtathletik
trade	Handel; Gewerbe
tradition	Tradition
traditional	traditionell
traffic light	Ampel
train	Zug
train station	Bahnhof
trainer	Turnschuh; Trainer/Trainerin
training	Training
to transport	transportieren
transport	Verkehrsmittel; Transport; Beförderung
to travel	reisen; fahren
travel agency	Reisebüro
treasure	Schatz
treasurer	Kassenwart/ Kassenwartin; Schatzmeister/ Schatzmeisterin
to treat	behandeln
tree	Baum
tribe	Stamm; Volksstamm
trick	Kunststück; Trick; Streich
trip	Fahrt; Ausflug; Reise
trouble	Schwierigkeiten; Problem; Ärger
trousers	Hose, Hosen
truck	Lastwagen (Lkw)
true	richtig; echt; richtig
to try	versuchen; probieren
T-shirt	T-Shirt
Tuesday	Dienstag
turkey	Truthahn; Pute
Turkish	Türkisch; türkisch; aus der Türkei
to turn	abbiegen; drehen
to turn around	(sich) umdrehen
to turn into	umwandeln in; verwandeln in
to turn off	ausschalten; abschalten
to turn on	einschalten
tutor	Klassenlehrer/ Klassenlehrerin
tutor time	Klassenstunde
TV	Fernsehen; Fernseher
twin	Zwilling
typical	typisch

U

umbrella	Regenschirm
unattended	unbeaufsichtigt
uncle	Onkel
under	unter
underground	unterirdisch; U-Bahn
to understand	verstehen
understood, understood	verstand, verstanden
unfair	unfair
unhappy	unglücklich
uniform	Uniform
university	Universität
until	bis
up	hinauf; nach oben; oben
us	uns; wir
US	US-amerikanisch
to use	benutzen; verwenden

useful	nützlich; hilfreich
useless	unbrauchbar

V

vacuum cleaner	Staubsauger
vegan	Veganer/Veganerin
vegetable	Gemüse
vegetarian	vegetarisch; Vegetarier/Vegetarierin
very	sehr
vice	Vize-
video	Video
view	Aussicht; Ausblick; Blick
Viking	Wikinger/Wikingerin
village	Dorf
vinegar	Essig
violence	Gewalt
violent	gewaltsam; gewalttätig; brutal
violin	Geige
visit	Besuch
to **visit**	besuchen
visitor	Besucher/Besucherin
voice	Stimme
volcano, volcanoes	Vulkan, Vulkane
volleyball	Volleyball
volunteer	Freiwilliger/Freiwillige; ehrenamtlicher Helfer/ehrenamtliche Helferin
to **vote**	wählen; abstimmen

W

to **wait (for)**	warten (auf)
waiter	Kellner
to **wake up**	aufwachen
Wales	Wales
walk	Spaziergang; Wanderung
to **walk**	laufen; gehen
wall	Wand; Mauer
wallpaper	Wandzeitung; Tapete
to **want (to)**	wollen
war	Krieg
wardrobe	Kleiderschrank
warm	warm
was	war
to **wash**	waschen
washing machine	Waschmaschine
waste	Abfall; Verschwendung
to **watch**	anschauen; ansehen; beobachten
water	Wasser
waterfall	Wasserfall
way	Weg; Art und Weise
we	wir
weapon	Waffe
to **wear**	tragen; anhaben
weather	Wetter
website	Website
Wednesday	Mittwoch
week	Woche
weekend	Wochenende
welcome (to)	willkommen (bei/in)
well	gut
Welsh	Walisisch; walisisch; aus Wales; Waliser/Waliserin
went	ging; fuhr
were	waren
west	Westen; westlich
wet	nass
wetland	Sumpfgebiet
whale	Wal
whale watching	Walbeobachten; Whalewatching
what	was; wie; welche
What about ...?	Was ist mit ...?
what else	was sonst; was noch
What's the matter?	Was ist los?; Was hast du?
wheelchair	Rollstuhl
when	wann; als; wenn
where	wo; wohin; woher
which	der/die/das; dem; den; welche
while	während
white	weiß *(soziale Kategorie)*
who	wer
whose	dessen; deren; wessen
why	warum
wide	breit
wilderness	Wildnis
wildfire	Lauffeuer; Flächenbrand

will	werden
to **win**	gewinnen
wind	Wind
window	Fenster
windy	windig
winner	Sieger/Siegerin; Gewinner/Gewinnerin
winter	Winter
to **wish**	wünschen
with	mit
without	ohne
woke up	wachte auf
wolf, wolves	Wolf, Wölfe
woman, women	Frau, Frauen
won	gewann, gewonnen
won't (= will not)	nicht werden
wonderful	wunderbar
wood	Holz; Wald
word	Wort
wore	trug; hatte an
work	Arbeit
to **work**	arbeiten; funktionieren
worker	Arbeiter/Arbeiterin
workshop	Workshop
world	Welt
worn	getragen; angehabt
to **worry**	sich Sorgen machen
worse, worst	schlimmer, schlimmste
would	würde
would like	würde(n) gern; hätte(n) gern
to **write**	schreiben
written	geschrieben
wrong	falsch
wrote	schrieb

X

xylophone	Xylophon

Y

yak	Yak
year	Jahrgangsstufe; Jahr
yearbook	Jahrbuch
yes	ja
yesterday	gestern
yet	schon; noch
yoga	Yoga
yoghurt	Joghurt
you	du; dir; dich; ihr; euch; Sie; Ihnen
You're welcome.	Gern geschehen.
young	jung
your	dein/deine; euer/eure; Ihr/Ihre
Yours,	Dein/Deine; Ihr/Ihre; Euer/Eure *(als Briefabschluss)*
yourself	dich; dich selbst
youth club	Jugendtreff
youth hostel	Jugendherberge
yummy	lecker

Z

zebra	Zebra
zoo	Zoo; Tierpark
zoom in	Heranzoomen

Quellennachweis

Abbildungen: Alamy stock photo, Abingdon (David South), **96.5**; Alamy stock photo, Abingdon (Glasshouse Images/JT Vintage), **121.2**; Alamy stock photo, Abingdon (Jack Sullivan), **85.6; 128.8**; Alamy stock photo, Abingdon (Mike Grandmaison / All Canada Photos), **70.1**; Alamy stock photo, Abingdon (Peter de Clercq), **29.2**; Alamy stock photo, Abingdon (PhotoStock-Israel / Ohad Shahar), **112.1**; Alamy stock photo, Abingdon (Richard Levine), **15.1**; Bláha, Marek, Offenbach am Main, **9.1; 9.2; 11.2; 13.1; 19.1; 23.1; 28.1; 29.1; 31.1; 34.5; 41.1; 52.1; 52.2; 53.1; 55.1; 55.2; 58.1; 58.2; 59.6; 63.1; 65.1; 66.1; 71.1; 74.1; 75.1; 75.2; 77.1; 77.2; 80.1; 87.1; 91.1; 93.1; 96.1; 97.1; 99.1; 99.2; 102.1; 102.2; 103.1; 104.1; 104.2; 107.5; 109.1; 120.1; 121.1; 129.5; 129.6**; CartoonStock Ltd, Bath (Baloo), **40.1**; Chudinskiy, Kirill, Köln, **35.1; 35.2; 35.3; 35.4; 35.5; 35.6**; Corel Corporation Deutschland, Unterschleissheim, **116.4**; dreamstime.com, Brentwood, TN (Ang Wee Heng John), **28.6**; Getty Images Plus, München (AGENZIA SINTESI / Alamy), **78.2**; Getty Images Plus, München (Ahmad Aji Prasetyo/iStock), **69.2**; Getty Images Plus, München (avid_creative), **130.20**; Getty Images Plus, München (Collection Mix: Subjects / Michael Nolan/robertharding), **73.1**; Getty Images Plus, München (Corbis Documentary / Layne Kennedy), **51.2**; Getty Images Plus, München (Diana Robinson Photography), **120.2**; Getty Images Plus, München (DigitalVision / EMS-FORSTER-PRODUCTIONS), **95.2**; Getty Images Plus, München (DigitalVision / Hill Street Studios), **124.3; 124.12**; Getty Images Plus, München (DigitalVision / Paul Souders), **68.1**; Getty Images Plus, München (DigitalVision / Riou), **102.5**; Getty Images Plus, München (DigitalVision/MoMo Productions), **34.4**; Getty Images Plus, München (DOMSTOCK/iStock), **69.1**; Getty Images Plus, München (E+ / Alex Potemkin), **65.2**; Getty Images Plus, München (E+ / doug4537), **50.2**; Getty Images Plus, München (E+ / dszc), **67.1**; Getty Images Plus, München (E+ / FrankRamspott), **50.1; 98.7**; Getty Images Plus, München (E+ / grandriver), **97.2**; Getty Images Plus, München (E+ / Hirurg), **62.1**; Getty Images Plus, München (E+ / LordHenriVoton), **98.6**; Getty Images Plus, München (E+ / SolStock), **129.1**; Getty Images Plus, München (E+/Ankit Sah), **39.5**; Getty Images Plus, München (E+/AzmanL), **76.7**; Getty Images Plus, München (E+/bkindler), **128.1**; Getty Images Plus, München (E+/Drazen_), **6.1**; Getty Images Plus, München (E+/eyecrave productions), **34.1**; Getty Images Plus, München (E+/FG Trade Latin), **78.3**; Getty Images Plus, München (E+/FG Trade), **41.2; 78.4**; Getty Images Plus, München (E+/Giselleflissak), **39.3**; Getty Images Plus, München (E+/kali9), **83.1; 89.1; 120.5**; Getty Images Plus, München (E+/kupicoo), **84.1; 85.5**; Getty Images Plus, München (E+/PeopleImages), **6.3; 78.1; 80.7**; Getty Images Plus, München (E+/RichLegg), **76.4**; Getty Images Plus, München (E+/RichVintage), **96.6**; Getty Images Plus, München (E+/SDI Productions), **32.1**; Getty Images Plus, München (E+/skynesher), **89.3**; Getty Images Plus, München (E+/yorkfoto), **30.5**; Getty Images Plus, München (Goodboy Picture Company/E+), **104.3**; Getty Images Plus, München (Image Source), **80.4**; Getty Images Plus, München (iStock / syolacan), **128.11**; Getty Images Plus, München (iStock/ Chesky_W), **108.1**; Getty Images Plus, München (Masterfile / Jeremy Woodhous), **76.5**; Getty Images Plus, München (Moment Open / Enzo Figueres), **19.3**; Getty Images Plus, München (Moment / Carmen Martínez Torrón), **68.2**; Getty Images Plus, München (Moment / Jia Liu), **72.2**; Getty Images Plus, München (Moment / Jultud), **54.5**; Getty Images Plus, München (Moment / Scott Suriano), **51.1**; Getty Images Plus, München (Moment/Anjelika Gretskaia), **76.1**; Getty Images Plus, München (Moment/Halfpoint Images), **34.2**; Getty Images Plus, München (Moment/Jasmin Merdan), **6.4; 7.1; 38.1**; Getty Images Plus, München (Moment/Jose A. Bernat Bacete), **39.1**; Getty Images Plus, München (Moment/Laura Olivas), **7.2; 56.1**; Getty Images Plus, München (Moment/the_burtons), **39.6**; Getty Images Plus, München (Monkey Business Images), **124.1**; Getty Images Plus, München (Photodisc / GeoStock), **67.4**; Getty Images Plus, München (Photodisc / Image Source), **21.2**; Getty Images Plus, München (SDI Productions), **124.11**; Getty Images Plus, München (SolStock/E+), **Cover.1**; Getty Images Plus, München (Stocktrek Images), **98.2**; Getty Images Plus, München (style-photography), **108.3**; Getty Images Plus, München (svetikd/E+), **122.11**; Getty Images Plus, München (Tatyana Aksenova / Tatyana Aksenova), **20.1**; Getty Images Plus, München (TerryJ), **96.3**; Getty Images Plus, München (The Image Bank / Danny Lehman), **8.5**; Getty Images Plus, München (The Image Bank / Siegfried Layda), **76.2**; Getty Images Plus, München (The Image Bank / Steve Prezant), **21.3**; Getty Images Plus, München (The Image Bank/David Zaitz), **39.4**; Getty Images Plus, München (thianchai sitthikongsak/Moment), **128.5**; Getty Images Plus, München (urbazon/E+), **112.3**; Getty Images Plus, München (valentinrussanov / E+), **42.1**; Getty Images Plus, München (1971yes / iStock), **130.1**; Getty Images, München (Ada Summer/Corbis/VCG), **7.3; 10.1**; Getty Images, München (Archive Photos / Kean Collection), **26.2**; Getty Images, München (Cavan / Regula Heeb-Zweifel), **18.2**; Getty Images, München (Corbis Historical / Stefano Bianchetti), **27.1**; Getty Images, München (Corbis Historical / Sunset Boulevard), **118.2**; Getty Images, München (Corbis / Robert Llewellyn), **111.3**; Getty Images, München (Corbis/Hal Beral), **95.1**; Getty Images, München (David Redfern), **118.1**; Getty Images, München (Gamma-Rapho / Patrick PIEL), **119.1**; Getty Images, München (Getty Images Entertainment / Frazer Harrison), **119.2**; Getty Images, München (Getty Images North America / Roy Rochlin), **10.2**; Getty Images, München (Icon Sportswire), **30.6**; Getty Images, München (Mint Images), **94.2**; Getty Images, München (MJ Zheng / 500px), **72.1**; Getty Images, München (Photographer's Choice RF / Richard Handwerk), **10.5**; Getty Images, München (Stone / Justin Lewis), **54.4**; Getty Images, München (Stone/Peter Unger), **76.6**; Getty Images, München (Tetra images / PT Images), **17.1**; Getty Images, München (Tetra Images), **27.2**; iStockphoto, Calgary, Alberta (babumani), **28.3**; iStockphoto, Calgary, Alberta (FatCamera), **120.7**; iStockphoto, Calgary, Alberta (iuliia_n), **48.3**; iStockphoto, Calgary, Alberta (LifeJourneys), **96.8**; iStockphoto, Calgary, Alberta (MasterLu), **24.1**; Klaus Hell, Essen, **85.4; 128.15**; Kramer, Peer, Schneverdingen, **44.1; 45.1; 45.2; 47.1; 47.2; 90.1**; Mauritius Images, Mittenwald (age fotostock), **37.7**; Mauritius Images, Mittenwald (Alamy Stock Photos / Jim West), **112.5**; Mauritius Images, Mittenwald (Alamy / Alpha Historica), **112.4; 114.2**; Mauritius Images, Mittenwald (Alamy / Beth Hall), **111.1**; Mauritius Images, Mittenwald (Alamy / CrackerClips Stock Media), **98.5**; Mauritius Images, Mittenwald (Alamy / Dennis Hallinan), **109.2**; Mauritius Images, Mittenwald (Alamy / Jeffrey Isaac Greenberg 7+), **105.1**; Mauritius Images, Mittenwald (Alamy / Jeffrey Isaac Greenberg 9+), **113.4**; Mauritius Images, Mittenwald (Alamy / Mark Stevens), **102.3**; Mauritius Images, Mittenwald (Alamy / Matthew Williams), **102.4**; Mauritius Images, Mittenwald (Alamy / Photo-fox) - Charles Clyde Ebbets „Lunch atop a Skyscraper" 1932, **12.1**; Mauritius Images, Mittenwald (Bob Daemmrich / Alamy), **124.10**; Mauritius Images, Mittenwald (Cavan Images), **30.1**; Mauritius Images, Mittenwald (dcphoto / Alamy), **115.1**; Mauritius Images, Mittenwald (FLHC JN8 / Alamy / Alamy Stock Photos), **25.1**; Mauritius Images, Mittenwald (Hanna Tor / Alamy), **30.4**; Mauritius Images, Mittenwald (Hansrad Collection / Alamy), **112.2**; Mauritius Images, Mittenwald (Jeffrey Isaac Greenberg 9+ / Alamy / Alamy Stock Photos), **18.5**; Mauritius Images, Mittenwald (Jim West), **30.2**; Mauritius Images, Mittenwald (JT Vintage), **113.1**; Mauritius Images, Mittenwald (Keith Jefferies / Stockimo / Alamy), **63.2**; Mauritius Images, Mittenwald (KGPA Ltd), **67.5**; Mauritius Images, Mittenwald (Lightspruch / Alamy), **111.4**; Mauritius Images, Mittenwald (Mark Sunderland Photography/Alamy), **128.12**; Mauritius Images, Mittenwald (Maryna Kolechyna / Alamy / Alamy Stock Photos), **18.1**; Mauritius Images, Mittenwald (Maskot), **102.8**; Mauritius Images, Mittenwald (mauritius images / William Morgan / Alamy), **111.2**; Mauritius Images, Mittenwald (Mytopshelf / Alamy), **67.3**; Mauritius Images, Mittenwald (nature picture library), **54.7; 98.1**; Mauritius Images, Mittenwald (Raga), **14.1**; Mauritius Images, Mittenwald (Ron Buskirk / Alamy), **111.5**; Mauritius Images, Mittenwald (Science Photo Library), **106.1**; Mauritius Images, Mittenwald (Tetra Images, LLC / Alamy Stock Photo), **34.3**; Mauritius Images, Mittenwald (Thislife pictures / Alamy / Alamy Stock Photos), **22.4**; Mauritius Images, Mittenwald (Thomas Haensgen), **10.4**; Mauritius Images, Mittenwald (TopFoto), **113.3**; Mauritius Images, Mittenwald (Westend61), **30.7**; Mauritius

Images, Mittenwald (Witold Skrypczak / Alamy), **67.7**; Mauritius Images, Mittenwald (World Book Inc.), **113.2**; Mauritius Images, Mittenwald (World History Archive / Alamy), **26.1**; Oser, Liliane, Hamburg, **6.2**; **6.5**; **8.3**; **10.6**; **11.1**; **16.1**; **16.2**; **30.3**; **54.3**; **57.1**; **57.2**; **57.3**; **57.4**; **57.5**; **57.6**; **59.1**; **59.2**; **59.3**; **59.4**; **59.5**; **76.3**; **98.3**; **100.1**; **100.2**; **100.3**; **100.4**; **101.1**; **101.2**; **101.3**; **101.4**; **107.6**; **107.7**; **107.8**; **123.1**; **123.2**; **123.3**; **123.4**; **123.5**; **123.6**; **123.7**; **126.1**; **126.2**; **126.3**; **126.4**; **126.5**; **126.6**; **126.7**; **126.8**; **126.9**; **126.10**; **126.11**; **126.12**; **126.13**; **126.14**; **127.7**; plainpicture GmbH & Co. KG, Hamburg (Bias), **67.6**; plainpicture GmbH & Co. KG, Hamburg (Carmen Spitznagel), **54.6**; plainpicture GmbH & Co. KG, Hamburg (Dave Wall), **18.4**; plainpicture GmbH & Co. KG, Hamburg (DEEPOL by plainpicture/Christian Vorhofer), **54.2**; plainpicture GmbH & Co. KG, Hamburg (DEEPOL by plainpicture/Konstantin Trubavin), **54.1**; plainpicture GmbH & Co. KG, Hamburg (DEEPOL by plainpicture), **58.3**; plainpicture GmbH & Co. KG, Hamburg (DEEPOL / Johan Alp), **102.7**; plainpicture GmbH & Co. KG, Hamburg (DEEPOL /Eva Blanco), **80.2**; plainpicture GmbH & Co. KG, Hamburg (DEEPOL/Maya Claussen), **120.9**; plainpicture GmbH & Co. KG, Hamburg (DEEPOL/Simona Pilolla), **89.4**; plainpicture GmbH & Co. KG, Hamburg (DEEPOL/Zero Creatives), **87.2**; plainpicture GmbH & Co. KG, Hamburg (DEEPOL/zerocreatives), **89.2**; plainpicture GmbH & Co. KG, Hamburg (DEEPOL), **93.2**; **102.6**; plainpicture GmbH & Co. KG, Hamburg (Design Pics/Carl Johnson), **73.2**; plainpicture GmbH & Co. KG, Hamburg (Design Pics/John Hyde), **8.6**; plainpicture GmbH & Co. KG, Hamburg (Design Pics/John Stubbs), **21.1**; plainpicture GmbH & Co. KG, Hamburg (Design Pics/Ken Gillespie), **8.1**; plainpicture GmbH & Co. KG, Hamburg (Design Pics/Yvonne Duivenvoorden), **39.2**; plainpicture GmbH & Co. KG, Hamburg (Frank Baquet), **19.2**; plainpicture GmbH & Co. KG, Hamburg (Jerry Monkman), **8.2**; plainpicture GmbH & Co. KG, Hamburg (Leander Hopf), **17.2**; plainpicture GmbH & Co. KG, Hamburg (Lena Granefelt), **8.7**; plainpicture GmbH & Co. KG, Hamburg (Marcus Windus), **18.3**; plainpicture GmbH & Co. KG, Hamburg (Michael Jonsson), **13.2**; plainpicture GmbH & Co. KG, Hamburg (Nordic Life/Terje Rakke), **67.2**; plainpicture GmbH & Co. KG, Hamburg (Patrick Strattner), **94.1**; plainpicture GmbH & Co. KG, Hamburg (p426m2309845), **98.4**; plainpicture GmbH & Co. KG, Hamburg (R. Schönebaum), **36.1**; plainpicture GmbH & Co. KG, Hamburg (Sibylle Pietrek), **10.3**; plainpicture GmbH & Co. KG, Hamburg (TOBSN), **Cover.2**; plainpicture GmbH & Co. KG, Hamburg (Valerie Schmidt), **64.1**; ShutterStock.com RF, New York (Africa Studio), **125.2**; ShutterStock.com RF, New York (Albina_Sol), **37.6**; ShutterStock.com RF, New York (AlessandroBiascioli), **125.6**; ShutterStock.com RF, New York (Alexander Kalina), **37.5**; ShutterStock.com RF, New York (Antonio Lopez Photography), **24.3**; ShutterStock.com RF, New York (Aryut Tantisoontornchai), **116.2**; ShutterStock.com RF, New York (Ben Gingell), **74.4**; ShutterStock.com RF, New York (BigPixel Photo), **120.8**; ShutterStock.com RF, New York (Billion Photos), **80.3**; ShutterStock.com RF, New York (BSG_1974), **85.2**; ShutterStock.com RF, New York (Cabeca de Marmore), **24.5**; ShutterStock.com RF, New York (Damian Lugowski), **37.2**; ShutterStock.com RF, New York (David Papazian), **122.8**; ShutterStock.com RF, New York (Dmitry Kalinovsky), **130.5**; ShutterStock.com RF, New York (Dotted Yeti), **108.2**; ShutterStock.com RF, New York (Er_On), **122.7**; ShutterStock.com RF, New York (Everett Collection), **28.8**; ShutterStock.com RF, New York (FeZsuPhoto), **125.3**; ShutterStock.com RF, New York (ff-photo), **37.3**; ShutterStock.com RF, New York (fizkes), **124.15**; ShutterStock.com RF, New York (Gorgev), **124.16**; ShutterStock.com RF, New York (Gorodenkoff), **70.2**; ShutterStock.com RF, New York (graficriver_icons_logo), **107.4**; ShutterStock.com RF, New York (Ground Picture), **127.5**; ShutterStock.com RF, New York (GTS Productions), **120.4**; ShutterStock.com RF, New York (Halfpoint), **127.4**; ShutterStock.com RF, New York (Have a nice day Photo), **130.19**; ShutterStock.com RF, New York (hxdbzxy), **128.18**; ShutterStock.com RF, New York (iacomino FRiMAGES), **28.9**; ShutterStock.com RF, New York (Icatnews), **128.3**; ShutterStock.com RF, New York (Inspired By Maps), **48.5**; ShutterStock.com RF, New York (itakdalee), **127.2**; ShutterStock.com RF, New York (Ivan Galashchuk), **70.3**; ShutterStock.com RF, New York (JabaWeba), **122.6**; ShutterStock.com RF, New York (Jacob Lund), **116.3**; ShutterStock.com RF, New York (jantsarik), **37.4**; ShutterStock.com RF, New York (Jaromir Chalabala), **116.5**; ShutterStock.com RF, New York (Jay Ondreicka), **105.2**; ShutterStock.com RF, New York (Jerry Gantar), **28.5**; ShutterStock.com RF, New York (JGPR), **128.14**; ShutterStock.com RF, New York (JoeSAPhotos), **32.2**; ShutterStock.com RF, New York (Kmpzzz), **129.3**; ShutterStock.com RF, New York (Krakenimages.com), **128.16**; ShutterStock.com RF, New York (Lazhko Svetlana), **49.1**; ShutterStock.com RF, New York (Le Do), **124.14**; ShutterStock.com RF, New York (Leigha Perales), **125.8**; ShutterStock.com RF, New York (LIGHTITUP), **92.1**; ShutterStock.com RF, New York (Lightspring), **129.4**; ShutterStock.com RF, New York (Lucky-photographer), **96.7**; ShutterStock.com RF, New York (magr80), **74.5**; ShutterStock.com RF, New York (Margaret.Wiktor), **92.2**; ShutterStock.com RF, New York (martinho Smart), **130.17**; ShutterStock.com RF, New York (matsabe), **107.2**; ShutterStock.com RF, New York (MBLifestyle), **130.4**; ShutterStock.com RF, New York (Mike Higginson), **122.5**; ShutterStock.com RF, New York (MilanMarkovic78), **128.7**; ShutterStock.com RF, New York (Miriam Doerr Martin Frommherz), **92.3**; ShutterStock.com RF, New York (Miss Janne), **107.3**; ShutterStock.com RF, New York (Monkey Business Images), **80.6**; **120.3**; **124.8**; **125.7**; **128.9**; ShutterStock.com RF, New York (Nagel Photography), **124.7**; ShutterStock.com RF, New York (Natasha Dorsey), **130.3**; ShutterStock.com RF, New York (NaturalVideographer), **74.6**; ShutterStock.com RF, New York (Neil Lockhart), **70.4**; ShutterStock.com RF, New York (New Africa), **125.4**; ShutterStock.com RF, New York (Nicku), **74.3**; ShutterStock.com RF, New York (Oleg Mikhaylov), **128.4**; ShutterStock.com RF, New York (Paolo Gallo), **124.4**; ShutterStock.com RF, New York (Paopano), **130.16**; ShutterStock.com RF, New York (PeopleImages.com - Yuri A), **124.2**; **125.11**; **128.10**; **129.2**; **130.12**; ShutterStock.com RF, New York (Peshkova), **122.2**; ShutterStock.com RF, New York (Peter Titmuss), **128.2**; ShutterStock.com RF, New York (Pickadook), **127.6**; ShutterStock.com RF, New York (Pixel-Shot), **124.5**; ShutterStock.com RF, New York (Pond Saksit), **125.5**; ShutterStock.com RF, New York (Popartic), **74.2**; ShutterStock.com RF, New York (Q3kiaPictures), **22.1**; **22.2**; **22.3**; ShutterStock.com RF, New York (RaiDztor), **122.12**; ShutterStock.com RF, New York (Ratchat), **122.10**; ShutterStock.com RF, New York (Rawpixel.com), **124.13**; ShutterStock.com RF, New York (Sergii Figurnyi), **24.4**; ShutterStock.com RF, New York (silverkblackstock), **92.4**; ShutterStock.com RF, New York (Smit), **80.5**; ShutterStock.com RF, New York (smolaw), **130.18**; ShutterStock.com RF, New York (Songquan Deng), **28.2**; ShutterStock.com RF, New York (sso4in), **130.10**; ShutterStock.com RF, New York (Stephen Moehle), **70.5**; ShutterStock.com RF, New York (Studio Romantic), **116.1**; ShutterStock.com RF, New York (Suzanne Tucker), **125.9**; ShutterStock.com RF, New York (Tatiana Buzmakova), **92.5**; ShutterStock.com RF, New York (Tristan3D), **130.9**; ShutterStock.com RF, New York (vandadorescu), **128.17**; ShutterStock.com RF, New York (Veroniksha), **128.20**; ShutterStock.com RF, New York (vipflash), **81.1**; ShutterStock.com RF, New York (wayfarerlife), **122.14**; ShutterStock.com RF, New York (wideonet), **48.1**; ShutterStock.com RF, New York (Xackery Irving), **13.3**; ShutterStock.com RF, New York (8 income), **122.13**; stock.adobe.com, Dublin (auspicious), **107.1**; stock.adobe.com, Dublin (Casa imágenes), **122.1**; stock.adobe.com, Dublin (Dreamframer), **37.1**; stock.adobe.com, Dublin (EKKAPON), **130.11**; stock.adobe.com, Dublin (Gerald Zaffuts), **114.1**; stock.adobe.com, Dublin (Grigory Bruev), **130.2**; stock.adobe.com, Dublin (Halfpoint), **130.8**; stock.adobe.com, Dublin (ImageFlow), **124.9**; stock.adobe.com, Dublin (insta_photos), **38.2**; stock.adobe.com, Dublin (Interstellar), **130.6**; stock.adobe.com, Dublin (JackF), **125.1**; stock.adobe.com, Dublin (JSirlin), **96.2**; stock.adobe.com, Dublin (lassedesignen), **130.14**; stock.adobe.com, Dublin (lovelyday12), **130.7**; stock.adobe.com, Dublin (Mark), **128.13**; stock.adobe.com, Dublin (Mary Perry), **125.12**; stock.adobe.com, Dublin (Michal), **122.3**; stock.adobe.com, Dublin (Otto Durst), **128.19**; stock.adobe.com, Dublin (Pormezz), **127.1**; stock.adobe.com, Dublin (pressmaster), **91.2**; stock.adobe.com, Dublin (Prostock-studio), **88.1**; **125.10**; stock.adobe.com, Dublin (sborisov), **8.4**; stock.adobe.com, Dublin (SeanPavonePhoto), **28.10**; stock.adobe.com, Dublin (shine), **124.6**; stock.adobe.com, Dublin (Stephen), **61.1**; stock.adobe.com, Dublin (Surachetsh), **122.9**; stock.adobe.com, Dublin (sveta), **85.3**; stock.adobe.com, Dublin (Svitlana), **128.6**; stock.adobe.com, Dublin (S.Kobold), **127.3**; stock.adobe.com, Dublin (thomaseder), **85.1**; stock.adobe.com, Dublin (tiero), **122.4**; stock.adobe.com, Dublin (Tryfonov), **120.6; 130.15**; Thinkstock, München (bhofack2), **48.2**; Thinkstock, München (comstock), **28.4**; Thinkstock, München (Comstock), **28.11**; Thinkstock, München (iStockphoto), **24.2; 48.4**; Thinkstock, München (SumikoPhoto), **96.4**; Thinkstock, München (Vacclav), **28.7**; www.CartoonStock.com, Bath (Jim Sizemore), **86.1**; 123rf Germany, c/o Inmagine GmbH, Nidderau (Christos Georghiou), **130.13**; © Digital Learning Associates Ltd 2019, **43.1; 43.2**

Text: Aus: Bundesministerium für Familie, Senioren, Frauen und Jugend, Berlin: Jugend stärken – Brücken in die Eigenständigkeit, 2022; Zur besseren altersgemäßen Verständlichkeit wurde der Originaltext verändert, ohne den Inhalt und/oder Sinn zu verändern., **64**; Fancy Dancer in: Ancestor Approved: Intertribal Stories for Kids ©2021 Monique Gray Smith; Zur besseren altersgemäßen Verständlichkeit wurde der Originaltext verändert, ohne den Inhalt und/oder Sinn zu verändern., **44-45**; From: Fancy Dancer in: Ancestor Approved: Intertribal Stories for Kids ©2021 Monique Gray Smith; Zur besseren altersgemäßen Verständlichkeit wurde der Originaltext verändert, ohne den Inhalt und/oder Sinn zu verändern., **47.1; 47.2**

Die Reihenfolge und Nummerierung der Bild- und Textquellen im Quellennachweis erfolgt automatisch und entspricht u. U. nicht der Nummerierung der Bild- und Textquellen im Werk. Die automatische Vergabe der Positionsnummern erfolgt in der Regel von links oben nach rechts unten, ausgehend von der linken oberen Ecke der Abbildung.